Praise for Denzil Meyrick:

'Absorbing . . . no run-of-the-mill tartan noir'
*The Times*

'Spellbinding . . . one of the UK's most loved crime writers'
*Sunday Post*

'Universal truths . . . an unbuttoned sense of humour
. . . engaging and eventful'
*Wall Street Journal*

'Satisfyingly twisted plot'
*Publishers Weekly*

'Touches of dark humour, multi-layered and compelling'
*Daily Record*

'Striking characters and shifting plots vibrate with energy'
*Library Journal*

'Compelling Scottish crime'
*Strand Magazine*

'If you like Rankin, MacBride and Oswald,
you'll love Meyrick'
*Sunday Mail*

'The right amount of authenticity . . . gritty writing
. . . most memorable'
*The Herald*

*A note on the author*

Denzil Meyrick was born in Glasgow and brought up in Campbeltown. After studying politics, he pursued a varied career including time spent as a police officer, freelance journalist and director of several companies in the leisure, engineering and marketing sectors. The bestselling DCI Daley thriller series includes: *Whisky from Small Glasses* (Waterstones Scottish Book of the Year, 2015), *The Last Witness, Dark Suits and Sad Songs, The Rat Stone Serenade, Well of the Winds, The Relentless Tide, A Breath on Dying Embers* and *Jeremiah's Bell*. Denzil lives on Loch Lomond side with his wife, Fiona.

# A LARGE MEASURE OF SNOW

## A TALE FROM KINLOCH

Denzil Meyrick

*Polygon*

First published in Great Britain in 2020 by Polygon, an imprint of Birlinn Ltd.

Birlinn Ltd
West Newington House
10 Newington Road
Edinburgh
EH9 1QS

www.polygonbooks.co.uk

1

ISBN  978 1 84697 557 8
eBook ISBN 978 1 78885 346 0

*British Library Cataloguing-in-Publication Data*
A catalogue record for this book is available on request from the British Library.

Typeset by 3btype.com

To the memory of Robert Black

*Was he an animal, that music could move him so?*
– *Metamorphosis*, Franz Kafka

# PROLOGUE

The gull was making for home through thick flurries of snow. It battled across the wind-tossed sound, before soaring high above the island at the head of the loch and out over the broad expanse of water that stretched before the small town.

Anyone staring up from the car on the east road to Firdale would have seen it. So would those cold, weary mariners on the ship battling through the grey waves seeking the safety of port, or the hill walker making her faltering way down the slippery slopes of Ben Saarnie. Even the curious seal, who popped her head out of the water just as it flew overhead, might have spied the creature and longed to take to the skies. To them and all who came before, there seemed nothing unusual about the bird, nothing unusual at all.

But this bird was the soul of the place.

Long it had watched over those who huddled around the shore of the sheltering loch. It had seen the first folk arrive, clad in skins and carrying spears. Then the ships with horsehead prows came. At first the people were scared of these strangers with tanned faces. But soon they marvelled at their possessions and the things they could do. Before long the wooden head of the horse became their totem.

It watched over them as they hunted and fished, and made

**1**

their first attempts to tame the land. It looked on in the time called the Bronze Age, as these busy folk laboured to erect their concentric rings and dig their ditches, fortified by shaven-spiked tree trunks at their hilltop strongholds. This was their defence against the others who lived beyond the gull's care. Some came from the sea, others the land. This was where his people climbed, seeking refuge from those who would do them harm.

The gull had seen the man in his fine shimmering breastplate and crimson plumed helmet as he gazed out across the short sea and dreamed of Hibernia. It watched as the men with the red hair arrived with their axes and swords. It flew over the dragon ships, their crews laying waste to all before them. Eventually, all of them settled, mixed and wed, melting away and becoming part of the community.

Over the years, it heard the tongue of its charges change. They gathered around blazing fires set to banish darkness and cold, their sweet songs of longing lilting on the night air. They sang first to the accompaniment of the shrill notes of reed whistles and then to the skirl of their pipes. It heard their words and stories, their poems of love, war and deep, desolate longing.

The gull had watched as small boats hollowed from logs and pitch became great ships of billowing sales, as hurdles became wheels on carriages drawn by shaggy ponies. These carriages soon propelled themselves, and before long the people could soar higher than the gull itself, horses almost forgotten.

It eyed the men in the dead of night, as they pushed casks with hoops, silenced by whispering wool, to boats on the shadowed quayside. It saw them slink back to their homes under the dull light of a waning moon, or the shaded flame of lamplight, only to emerge bold and tall under the sparkling sun of the new day.

The gull saw men go to war – many times they went to war. At first they donned the plaid woven in rough cloth, as had their ancestors. They battled men clad in steel; they battled men clad only in the paint that covered their bodies. But still they survived through the ages.

Then men in crimson coats with their sticks of fire and flashing swords came. The bird lowered its head as souls marched off in the dun suits of destruction, heading for battlefields far, far away, of which it knew nothing. It wondered why they fought as, in time, it had to turn its head away, too sad to see the women and children weep their tears of desperation for lost loves and dead fathers. It, too, mourned those destined never to return to the loch that was their home, or back into its care.

When the iron bird flew over the town and brought death and terror, the gull watched as the people huddled in the hills that had always been their strength. It looked down as great grey warships, the descendants of the dragon boats of long ago, filled the loch.

It swooped over the ring-net fishing fleet as they took on the great waves, in tiny boats of ancient line. There were the women on the pier packing salted silver herrings into wooden barrels. It caught the scent of peat, malt and burning coal before the sweet tang of raw spirit flowed like clear, clear water from keen copper stills.

When men came to the hill where once had stood the fort of rings and sharpened logs, to remove the black jet necklace from the ground and encase it in a glass box, out of time and place, the gull could remember the day the king who had worn it so proudly was put to rest in the dark earth, and how the folk had wept. But those tears, like many before and those yet to come, had been and would be forgotten.

And now, from his vantage point high on the hill, the seagull watched over a busy little place of homes, streets, shops and chimneys. Boats still set off to sea, men mined for coal, whisky still flowed, farmers tilled the soil as the seasons turned, and the horseless cars meandered like tireless ants. Women still wept for lost loves and ruined lives, and children still cried, bewildered by absences they could not yet fathom.

The bird tucked his head under one wing against the snow. Perched on one yellow leg, he wondered what would come next for the people he had watched over, seen but unseen, for so long.

# 1

*Kinloch, December 1967*

The group of old men huddled in the shelter of the Mission to Seamen that stood sentinel before the harbour at Kinloch. For most of them, having plied their trade at the fishing for a lifetime, inclement weather was no obstacle to standing in the elements having a yarn. But today was different.

As they looked on from under screwed-down bunnets, Breton caps or the odd sou'wester, the scene before them could best be described as being *unusual*, in terms of the prevailing weather of the south Kintyre peninsula. Snow was falling, and it was falling hard. Not only that, it had the impertinence to have already coated just about everything in sight with a white blanket. The palm trees that sprouted along the pier road, testaments to the mighty Atlantic Drift that normally cosseted the inhabitants of Kinloch in an unnaturally benign climate, had been defiled. Now they stood like exotic Christmas trees, frosted by the adorning flakes.

Along the esplanade, all but one bollard wore a white peak like a witch's hat, the only exception being the one near the roundabout, where Isa McKechnie had taken a tumble and landed on it only a few minutes before, flattening the snow like a pan scone. She had been helped to her feet by the passing Reverend McNee, who declared that he had prayed the snow would stop before he took the long and winding road to Glasgow later that day.

At the head of the quay, a light blue Hillman Minx now wore a white roof. Beside it, Michael Kerr the Baker's van bore the legend 'YOUR CAKES ARE SHITE' in the accumulated snow on its windscreen. The culprit, young Derek Paterson, sacked as a Saturday boy at the bakery for clandestinely eating four Danish pastries and some meringues, had been unable to resist the temptation as he passed by on the way to school.

The snowflakes were even fatter and more numerous now than they had been in the previous hour, and the rigging of boats hung heavy white, as did the roof of the harbour master's office, the weigh house, fuel tanks and the fish buyer's new Rover 2000. The latter had been denounced as flash by the maritime fraternity and, in any case, would soon be tainted by that particular scent peculiar to the fruits of the sea.

Being a practical man, Sandy Hoynes had squeezed his bulky frame into oilskins that would have been a perfect fit a decade ago. Now, he looked like a purposeful lemon as he trod gingerly from the *Girl Maggie* moored at the pier and headed towards the gathering by the Mission. However, their collective attention was not fixed on his progress, but on a seagull that was leaving marks with its webbed feet in the snow on the pavement before them. Donald McKirdy swore blind they were spelling out 'The end is nigh', though none of his companions could discern this. The gull eyed them all with disdain before taking off into the pearlescent sky with a loud squawk of derision, ejecting a watery deposit that landed on Hoynes' left wellington boot. Fortunately, the silencing quality of snow disguised the profanity that issued from Hoynes' mouth as he took to the road.

'Aye, I'm sure yous have only one date in mind,' he said, as he approached the group of men he knew so well.

'Nineteen forty-seven,' came back in ragged unison. For that year had seen the worst snow in living memory, sending the town into isolation and its citizens into a flurry of activity. The west road had been blocked at Muirloan for three whole weeks, and it was even longer before the bus could make its way back to Firdale up the twists and turns of the treacherous eastern way.

But the good folk of Kinloch and the villages thereabouts knew that they could weather any storm that blocked roads, because they had an ancient highway on their doorstep: the sea. Boats of all descriptions were despatched hither and thon to collect the necessities of life. They had plenty coal from the mine at Machrie to keep them warm and an elegant sufficiency of food to fill their bellies. So life continued much as normal. This general contentment prevailed despite the inevitable loss of electricity that rendered modern contraptions like electric light useless. It also caused a rush on Rory McQuinn's store in Main Street as those in search of the replenishment of accumulators harried the shopkeeper. And even now, all these years later, the same shop was doing a rare trade in batteries. For the people of Kinloch loved the wireless, and some could barely imagine how life had been without it. Television – well, that was something else altogether – and despite missing *The Andy Stewart Show*, in their opinion, there was little else to bother about.

Peeny, for that was his nickname, scratched the end of his sharp nose. 'Aye, it's the same all over again. Man, I'm fair glad

I've no' to make sail for the Ayrshire coast in this. It's a blessing that my days in the wheelhouse are done.' Then, in a more reflective tone: 'But mind you, I've tae listen to my dear Elspeth all day now, and that's a task any decent man would find daunting.'

His companions nodded in silent agreement, for most of them had been at the wrong end of the said Elspeth's tongue at one time or another. But, on a positive note, she was well known for her skills as a cook. They'd all sampled her mince and tatties, undoubtedly the best around. Though none would dare admit it to their own wives lest they be accused of something much more damning than marital infidelity.

'It's set for the day, and no mistake,' said Hoynes. 'You wait, the cry will be out for those of us that are left to take to the sea and feed the toon.' He stared mournfully at the loch before him. He'd not long been skipper of the *Girl Maggie* the last time such a calamity had hit. In those days fishing boats sat in rows, filling in the gap between the twin piers with no room to spare. Now, these vessels populated only half of the harbour. A sad reflection on the times, he thought.

As though picking up on these thoughts, Malcolm Connelly sighed. 'Aye, you youngsters will be fair inundated by errands of mercy if this is as bad as it was back then. And precious little thanks you'll get for your endeavours, neither.'

Sandy Hoynes liked to be called a youngster, even though, now in his early sixties, he was the second oldest skipper in the fleet. 'Och, we'll just have to manage. But it will need to be better arranged this time round, that's for sure. Though here's hoping this is just a wee minding. Hamish says it will be fair melted away by the afternoon. And as yous all know, he has the sight.'

This statement was greeted by a general murmur of what could best be described as scepticism, as white clouds of breath billowed out from the little crowd only to be punctured numerously by flurries of snow.

'Come on, Sandy,' said McKirdy. 'Does it look to you as though this will stop any time soon? Take a gander at the sky, man. It's fair heavy – fit to burst, no less. By this afternoon, it's mair likely to be a blizzard.'

This suggestion seemed to meet with greater approval than Hamish's meteorological prophecies, so Hoynes decided to say no more on the subject. 'There's little point in us all loitering here, gathering the white stuff. Look at Peeny; he's damn near a snowman as it is. We'll head up to the County and see if the auld fella will serve us a dram a wee bit before time – for medicinal use against the cold, you understand. I'm sure it's lawful for a fisherman to seek refreshment at any moment in weather like this.'

'And even if it's not, that bugger won't turn doon twelve good men and true wae a few shillings in their pockets,' Peeny remarked, as he brushed snow from his shoulders.

Like a murmuration of starlings, as one, the little band of men turned and set off up the hill to the warmth and solace of the County Hotel. For today was a day for drams and yarns beside a roaring fire, not al fresco weather-watching.

If they had been birds, they could have soared high enough to take in a scene more akin to an alpine village than a small fishing town on the west coast of Scotland. And though it bore its own beauty, it brought danger.

And still the snow fell.

# 2

That Hamish was out to impress was obvious to all who knew the man. For a start, the quiff of dark hair that sprung from an increasingly large expanse of forehead was oiled back to perfection. Those in the know would have instantly noted that stray ear hairs – an unfortunate family trait – had been pared back so that they couldn't be viewed when looking at his face front on.

The best indication as to his intention to impress was what he wore. He was dressed in the suit his late father had bought in 1951 for a wedding. Though it fitted him passably well – both father and son were by nature lean – his mother had taken the best part of the morning to convince him that it was still in style.

'Och, Hamish, I never took you for a gentleman o' vanity,' she chided. 'Ask Jimmy Bryson the tailor – good clothes never go out of fashion.'

But as he stared at himself in the wardrobe mirror, he saw the elderly insurance man who came to collect his mother's contributions every week, rather than the trendy man-about-town image he'd hoped to project.

'And anyway,' his mother continued, 'it's no' as though you're in the first flush of youth. If it's a wife you're trying to snag, well, you better make it quick before what hair you have is left on the pillow. Your father was the same, as was his before him. Your grandda was a right thrawn old bugger intae the bargain. Sat in the County telling his tales, waiting for someone to buy him a dram. Promise me you won't end your days like him, Hamish. It's no credit to a man.'

'You married into the family,' said Hamish, with a hint of indignation.

'Aye, well, it was between the wars, and us women in the town weren't exactly spoilt for choice. And your father was a well-doing soul . . . until the bottle became his best friend, that is.'

Hamish knew this only too well. The family had lost their fishing boat because of his father's enthusiasm for whisky. It was a hobby that killed him not long after. Had it not been for the generosity of spirit of Sandy Hoynes, who took him on as first mate, Hamish had no idea where he'd have ended up. A life down the pit at Machrie or across in the shipyard where the noise was sufficient to frighten the dead were the most likely options. It was a thought that often made him shudder.

But he felt no ill will towards his father. He knew himself the pull of a convivial dram. But he was as determined to master it as he was to make an impression this day. 'I have my sights set high, Mother. My father might be dead, and my grandfather a miserable old bugger cadging drinks in the bar at the County, but that's not me.'

'Well, I'll no' be here to find oot. But you have a look of your grandfather, and no mistake. I see it more every day as your hair falls out. It's across the eyes – there's a right slant to them.'

'Will you stop with the hair and the eyes! I'm getting one o' they complexes.'

'Don't be so dramatic. If there's one thing a woman doesn't like, it's a man with a favour for exaggeration.'

'Anyway, I never mentioned a woman.'

'Well, if you're all dressed up to meet Sandy Hoynes, I'm worried.'

'If you must know, I'm to be interviewed for the *Glasgow Times*. They're doing a piece on young fishermen from around the country.'

'And they chose you?' Hamish's mother looked momentarily taken aback.

'Well, not right at the start, no. Duncan O'May was their first choice, but he caught the chickenpox last week.'

'Oh well, that was lucky.'

'Then they went for Archie Robertson, but he's self-conscious because of that stutter.'

'But he's a fine-looking boy, great heid of hair tae, and no mistake. So you were the third choice?'

'No' exactly.' Hamish screwed up his face. 'They were keen on Alex Morrans, but he got the jail at the weekend for fighting with Bobby Johnson and he's no' out till the hearing on Friday when the Sheriff gets here.'

'Dear me, we're running out of young fishermen.' She raised her eyes to the ceiling.

'Sandy put me forward. Said it would be great to have me in the papers representing a fine craft like the *Girl Maggie*.'

'Oh aye, like the *Queen Mary*, so she is.'

'Mother, as fishing boats go, there's not a better sail in the fleet.'

'I daresay, but she looks like a tramp's underpants.'

'Sandy doesna believe in style over substance, Mother. He says it's a working vessel. We're serious fishermen, no' they day-sailors who're just after prettification.'

'Well, he's certainly succeeded in that desire. Aye, and you're starting to sound like him. I'd guard against that if I were you. For folk from Kinloch to Copenhagen know fine what a rogue the man is.'

'He is not! He's always been fair to me, and I'll not forget him for it. And I'm proud to have my photograph taken in front of his fishing boat. Proud as punch, and no mistake.'

'Aye, well, jeest don't give it any of that second-sight stuff to the reporter. That's another trait you take from your grandda.'

'Och, wheesht, Mother.' Hamish took one last look at himself in the mirror. 'Right, that's me off to meet Joe.'

'Joe who?'

'Joe Baird. He's the journalist from the *Glasgow Times*. His secretary phoned Sandy last night at his house.'

'Aye, good luck. You'll need it in all this snow.'

'Och, it'll make the pictures look fair dramatic, so it will.'

'Aye, if you say so, son.'

❄

Hamish wished he'd worn his thick pea jacket against the elements as he took the short cut from his mother's flat in the Glebe Fields down the distillery lane. By the time he'd turned into Long Road, his feet were freezing in his good Sunday shoes, and he was huddled into the old suit that offered little protection against the heavy snow.

It didn't take him long to get to the café in the centre of

Kinloch, though on the way, even with the camouflage of a thick coating of snow, his wearing of a suit was noted and remarked upon by the locals. Jean McNaughton thought he might be heading for court, while old Peter Carmichael was sure he was after a job interview at the new clothes factory.

'Don't be so ridiculous, Peter,' said Jean indignantly. 'If it's a job at the new clothing factory he's after, he would hardly be heading there in a suit that's damn near twenty years old. What kind of impression would that make?'

Peter nodded sagely. He could see the reasoning in this. 'Wait, he's stopped.'

Despite the deepening snow, Hamish was standing in front of the florist, checking his reflection in the window; he dallied for a few moments, brushing snow from his suit and checking his quiff was still intact.

'It's a woman!' said Jean with surprise.

'No, not Hamish. If he ever had any notions of a wife, the confidence to ask a lassie oot will have been well and truly sooked out of him by that mother of his. She could turn whisky sour.'

'A shilling on it, if you're so confident.'

'Sixpence!'

'Right, you're on!' Jean rubbed her mittened hands together. 'I'll get some nice sausages from young Alastair the butcher as a treat when I win.'

'Oh aye. He might be no mair than a lad, but he's a genius wae a sausage, and no mistake.'

They looked on intently as Hamish pushed open the door to the café.

# 3

The gimlet-eyed proprietor of the County Hotel watched them with a furrowed brow when they arrived. But the prospect of a parcel of fishermen in funds, spending what promised to be a bad day for business in front of his fire, was a tempting one.

Soon, oilskins, bunnets and sou'westers were left hanging on the coat stand in the lobby, while the men who'd worn them sat bathing in the warmth of the coal fire in the bar.

'Aye, but is that not a fine feeling?' said Peeny, as melting snow dripped from the end of his nose. 'Whoot more is there in life but a good fire on a winter's day, fine conversation and a dram in your fist?'

'A larger dram would be an improvement,' Hoynes remarked from his seat right in front of the flames. 'But I have to say, there is a certain conviviality aboot it all, nonetheless.'

The proprietor leaned against the bar. 'Don't you all be of the notion that this is jeest a port in a storm. These seats have to be paid for. You're not all filling up places customers willing to put their hands in their pockets will be looking for come lunchtime.'

'Who do you think will brave the weather to come out on a day like this?' said McKirdy. 'They'd have to be bereft of mind.'

With that, the front door swung open, bringing with it an icy draught. Hamish stood framed in the entrance, his suit plastered in snow and his quiff white and sticking up like one of the new-fangled ice-cream cones they'd been selling at Gino's café.

'There you have it,' said McKirdy. 'I'm right. Would you look at this apparition! Fair wanting in the heid to be out in this without so much as a toorie.'

'Ach, leave the boy alone,' said Hoynes. 'Young folk these days are fair filled with ideas that oor generation canna get a handle on. I mean, who'd have thought that there'd be men walking aboot with hair the length of a lassie's, and the lassies themselves turned oot with barely a skirt on at all?'

'Aye, you're right, Sandy,' said Peeny. 'It's worse things is getting, tae. My nephew arrived hame the other night and produced one of they joints.'

McKirdy looked confused. 'Whether it was beef, lamb or pork, there's nothing to be sniffed at aboot a joint, surely?'

'Naw, not that kind of joint! The one you see these days wae the guitars smoking. Whoot do they call it?'

'Silly shag?' said Jim McMichael.

'Ach, away! It's the wacky baccy they're calling it. You wouldna put that stuff in a decent briar pipe,' said Hoynes.

'Well, he lit up right in front o' my sister Jean. Of course, she didna have a clue whoot was afoot, but I could smell it straightaway.'

'How do you recognise it?'

'Was I no' at that accordion and fiddle club ceilidh last month. They musicians are all at it.'

'No' wee Roger surely, he's only a boy!' said McKirdy.

'No' him. But I'm telling you, I recognise the odour; it's

right particular, so it is.' He crossed his arms to make the point, as the rest of the assembled fishermen looked into the flames and tried to picture the members of the Kinloch and District Fiddle and Accordion club partaking in forbidden substances.

'It's this "tune in and drop out" – they're all at it. I saw it on the news. Well, I'm here to tell you, the last time I heard old McGeachy at the fiddle he might have dropped oot, but he certainly hadn't tuned in. Fair wailing, it was,' said Hoynes.

'Mind you, it's no' a patch on a good dram,' said Peeny.

'Man, you didna partake in a draw yourself, did you?'

Peeny sat back in his chair with his hands behind his head. 'Aye, well, whoot does a man's journey through life mean if he's no' willing to take a new path?'

They all turned to look at him, mouths agape.

'But it has to be said that while I got a wee sensation, it was only fleeting. After it, my mouth tasted like a Bedouin's sandal.' The thought prompted him to take his baccy from his pocket and tamp some down in the bowl of his pipe with a thumb.

'Maybe I'll gie it a go myself,' said Andy Duncan, at ninety the oldest present.

'I widna be in a rush to be doing that, Andy. I'm sure we had to get the ambulance for you last year when you had one o' they Babychams,' said Hoynes.

'It wisna that at all,' said McKirdy. 'The man drank near a bottle o' Johnnie Walker before he had a glass o' that stuff. They'd to rinse his liver oot wae a mangle.'

The old man looked McKirdy squarely in the face and raised his withered middle digit by way of a reply.

'Hamish, brush yourself doon, man. You'll catch your death encased in all that snow,' said Hoynes in an avuncular manner.

'And when you've done that, I'd be fair grateful for a dram. It's a skipper's privilege. One day you'll be asking the same of your crew. Just for me, mind. This parcel of rogues can dip in their ain pockets. Aye, and be sure to get yourself one while you're at it, before we need tae send for one o' they big dogs from the Alps. The creatures wae the wee barrels strung through their collars.'

'Saint Bernards,' said Hamish.

'I'm no' right sure who they belong to, but I've always fancied bumping into one,' said Hoynes. 'But if they do belong to this saint, he's got no business encouraging folk to partake in alcohol. There's nothing Christian aboot that, at all.'

'Unless you're the Reverend McSorley,' said Peeny.

'Aye, but he gets dispensation to be half cut most of the day on account of him being blown up at Monte Cassino wae the Argylls,' opined Alex Watson, who'd only just thawed out enough to be able to speak.

'Aye, he got blown up right enough. But he must have landed in a cask o' wine, for he's no' been oot his cups since,' said old Andy Duncan.

'Well, here's hoping he doesna take to the Babycham,' said Hoynes. 'The ambulance will be fair rushed off its feet.'

Amidst the laughter, and having brushed most of the snow from his suit, Hamish tapped Hoynes on the shoulder. 'Can I have a word with you, skipper?'

'There's no need tae whisper, Hamish. We're amongst friends here,' he said loudly. Then in a quieter voice: 'It's no' aboot that wee favour I did for Mrs McKay, is it?'

Hamish shook his head.

'Aye, well, spill what's on your mind, Hamish.' Hoynes was back to his ebullient self. 'Oh, and while you're at it, you can maybe tell me why you're all dressed up in your faither's suit? May he rest in peace.'

'Sure you know, I've been speaking to the *Glasgow Times*, remember?'

'Och, that's right enough,' said Hoynes, grabbing Hamish's arm. 'They've chosen oor Hamish here to represent young fishermen everywhere. The *Glasgow Times*, no less.'

'Aye, after they went round just aboot the whole fleet asking everybody else,' said McKirdy. 'And you're no spring chicken, neither, Hamish. You must be pushing thirty, if you're a day.'

'Wheesht, McKirdy,' said Hoynes. 'Let my man speak.'

'The reporter has asked us a favour, Sandy,' said Hamish.

'And what might that be?'

'Well, it's a case of wondering if we'll be heading off tae bring supplies for the toon from across on the Ayrshire coast. I let on that it sometimes happens in times of snow like this.'

'And you did right! My, tae see the *Girl Maggie* featured in the *Glasgow Times* as she braves the elements tae save Kinloch would be a fair spectacle. What do you think, men?'

'I'd gie her a lick o' paint, if I were you,' said McKirdy waspishly.

'In this weather? No' likely. The *Girl Maggie* is a working vessel, no' some pleasure cruiser. She'll be pictured as she is – a brave wee boat, working hard to save the people of Kinloch from fair starving to death. It's an honour.'

This was greeted by a disaffected murmur.

'A round of drinks for my friends to celebrate!' Hoynes smiled beatifically at his colleagues, old and young.

'Och, maybe it's not a bad thing, right enough,' said Peeny. 'A wee boost for the fleet will do it the world of good. Make mine a malt – by way of celebration, you understand.'

Hoynes gazed at him malevolently for a moment, then drew his attention back to his first mate. 'This reporter, what's his name?'

Hamish shuffled uncomfortably from foot to foot. 'Baird, the reporter's name is Baird. Aye, and here's a down payment, a kind of retainer, you understand. We'll get the full sum when the job's done.' He fished out a large white five-pound note from his pocket.

Hoynes grabbed it like a flytrap. 'Well, now, you see. Isn't that a sight to behold? A fine man this Baird must be, right enough.' He pocketed the fiver with relish.

Beside him, Hamish's face bore a pained, some might say anguished expression.

# 4

The snow didn't stop for the rest of that day, nor through the night. When first light dawned, the sky was bright, but to the east more ominous clouds were gathering battalions of snowflakes in good order, ready to march on Kinloch.

As predicted the previous day, the Glasgow road was snowbound, and the good people of the town were indeed cut off from the rest of civilisation. The unfortunate Reverend McNee had been forced to seek shelter from the snow halfway between Kinloch and Glasgow at Inveraray.

The town itself had taken on an altogether different aspect. Houses, once with sharply defined gabled roofs, looked more akin to bakers' loaves. Every angle had been softened under the thick snow, and if anyone acquainted with the familiar silhouettes had been presented with this new spectacle, they wouldn't have recognised the place. Fences could barely be seen. Sheep looked a dirty white against the virgin snow. The council's gritting lorry had long since given up the ghost, stuck fast as it was at the top of the Still Brae. Shops, though staying open, boasted only a trickle of customers, wrapped up in so many hoods, hats and scarves as to make them unidentifiable. This was something of a novelty for the community, where everyone knew everyone else. The new pastime of working out who was who under each great huddle of clothes was both intriguing and unsettling.

An emergency meeting of Kinloch's town council was in session in the wood-panelled chamber in the town hall. Its members sat around a huge, polished mahogany table, each face etched with concern.

'I'm minded to hold my hand out to our brave fishing community,' said Francis McMurdo, the town's provost and senior politician. 'They came through for us in nineteen forty-seven, and I'm sure they'll rise to the occasion again.'

Jessie McCorkindale looked less optimistic. 'Aye, and you'll recall the bad feeling that emerged after that. The shopkeepers gave them the bare minimum then doubled the price of everything. There was damn near a revolution!'

'Well, I have no special powers to force fishermen or shopkeepers to bend the knee to any of the ideas put in place by this council. We can only appeal to the better nature of all those involved.'

There was a general air of scepticism around the table at this remark. For memory was long in Kinloch, and an un-righted wrong was bound to have consequences even two decades on.

'I suggest we declare a state of emergency and call in the army,' said Councillor Galbraith. 'Get them on the boats at gunpoint, if necessary.'

McMurdo eyed him as he puffed on his pipe. 'There's a few flaws in that notion, Jamie. For one, if the army could get here, they'd be able to bring supplies themselves. And secondly, even if we could avail ourselves of their services, you'll remember the riots we had on our hands when they redcaps came during the war to arrest that local lad who went AWOL.'

'They flung them in the loch!' hooted Alec Macmillan, often one of the more obdurate members around the table. 'And in any case, the idea of forcing men to sea in what could be life-threatening circumstances is reckless in the extreme. You'd have a terrible load to deal with if only a fraction of the fleet returned, and no mistake.'

'The lives of the whole community will be at risk if we can't get any food from somewhere,' said the provost. 'The Co-op's running low, and the same goes for just about every shop in the town. Of course, folk are panic buying. I saw the widow Munro this very morning with a shopping basket of sugar that would have sweetened every cup of tea of a battalion on the move.'

'Could we not commandeer the boats if the fishermen don't toe the line?' said Galbraith.

'I'm glad you're not the provost, Jamie. You'd make auld Joe Stalin look like the fairy godmother,' said McMurdo.

An argument ensued, with everyone round the table talking heatedly at once.

Banging his gavel, Provost McMurdo brought the committee – with no little difficulty – to order. 'There is one ray of hope, mind you.'

The warring factions around the table ceased hostilities, as every eye turned to the man in the provost's chair.

'This came through my door this morning.' McMurdo waved a sheet of paper.

'What is it, peace in our time?' Macmillan sneered.

'No. It's a missive from Sandy Hoynes. He must have put it through my door last night, for it was on the mat first thing this morning.'

The very mention of Hoynes engendered the odd raised eyebrow and a few grunts of disaffection.

Undaunted, McMurdo continued. 'He and his boat are to be featured in the *Glasgow Times*, no less. He tells me, and I quote, "It would give me the greatest pride imaginable to be part of the effort to keep the good people of Kinloch, who are so close to my heart, fed and watered at this difficult time." I have to say I was quite moved.'

'He hasn't told you what he's after yet,' said Macmillan. 'If I know him, the price will be his own weight in whisky. And in any case, it's only one boat. That'll feed no more than a few families if we're lucky.'

'Well, I think we should accept his offer of assistance. Indeed, highlighting our plight in the *Glasgow Times* will do no harm as far as letting people know in what straitened times we find ourselves here in Kinloch. And anyway, the rest of the fleet will follow Hoynes. You know how competitive they all are.'

Despite the numerous doubts of those gathered, it was agreed that the council assist Sandy Hoynes in his endeavours with every resource at their disposal.

As McMurdo brought the meeting to a close, he thanked his fellow councillors and the proposal was passed. 'I know, while in some quarters he is considered to be—'

'Fly as buggery,' said Macmillan, finishing the provost's sentence for him.

'I would rather say . . . some remain to be convinced.' He turned to the clerk. 'Please strike Mr Macmillan's comment from the minutes, Mr McIntyre.' He stared up at the chamber windows. 'But in times like this, beggars can't be choosers.'

Outside, more fat flakes were falling on Kinloch.

# 5

Having managed to avail himself of the authority of the town council via a unanimous vote, Provost McMurdo was now picking his way through the snowdrift on Main Street towards the quay. He was pleased they'd managed to reach something approaching consensus. What swung it had been the intervention of the local association of innkeepers, who foretold that beer, whisky and just about every other form of alcohol would be exhausted in less than a week. It appeared that it was not only sugar that was being hoarded by the community.

McMurdo crossed the roundabout at the pierhead, almost immediately spying the rotund figure of Hoynes in his yellow oilskins aboard the *Girl Maggie*. A few stumbles and no little effort brought him athwart the vessel, where it looked as though Hoynes was busy with a paintbrush.

'Good morning, Sandy,' said McMurdo, checking his watch to ensure that noon hadn't yet turned.

'Ahoy there, provost,' said Hoynes. 'It's a lovely day, is it not? Apart from the snow, that is.'

'Aye, the sky is bright enough now, but that cloud is almost upon us, and it looks heavy-laden with snow to me.'

'Ach, jeest passing. You'll no' see any snow this day. Though it'll be blizzards up near the Rest. It could take weeks to open the road.' He sniffed the air like a dog. 'Remember, if you want to be sure o' the weather, never heed that nonsense on the wireless, just ask a fisherman. Well, one of my vast experience, at any rate.'

'I hope you're right,' said McMurdo, looking doubtfully heavenward.

'I take it you received my wee note last night?'

'Aye, I did, Sandy. A very generous offer it is, too. In fact, I've been in session with the council and the trade association since early this morning. The town clerk is negotiating an accommodation with the shopkeepers, but I think you'll find the outcome will be favourable.' He looked at the sky again. 'Of course, you'll be in receipt of a fine reward from the *Glasgow Times*, I'm quite sure, Sandy.'

'Och, not a bit of it! There's been the usual undertakings, but no hard cash has changed hands nor been agreed,' said Hoynes, ignoring the fact that the five-pound note was sitting, tightly folded, in his wallet up in the wheelhouse. 'But if it means feeding the starving and putting Kinloch on the map, who am I to say no, eh?'

McMurdo raised an eyebrow. 'I'm sure you know your own business, Sandy.'

'Aye, and fair thin times for business they are, right enough.'

'Well, we'll have an offer for you and the rest of the fleet before five o'clock. It's hoped you'll be able to put to sea tomorrow morning.'

Hoynes rubbed his chin and looked at the sky with a leery eye. 'I daresay we could do that. Mind you, I canna speak for my fellow skippers. As you're aware, they're a right thrawn outfit at the best o' times.'

'I'm sure the chance to make some money in the run-up to Christmas will be enough to change their mind. In any event, the pubs and shops are already running short of beer, whisky and the like. As you know, today is normally the brewers' delivery day. And that's not going to happen.'

'Damn me!' said Hoynes, suddenly feeling the need to reach for his pipe and baccy. 'There must be a few sore heads today if the stocks are running down so far!'

'I'm afraid some people have been stockpiling. Very selfish – human nature at its worst in a time of crisis.'

'These folk will answer for it in the next world, and that's for sure!' said Hoynes, as the wad of tobacco in the bowl of his pipe glowed red amidst the white all around.

The provost turned. A young lad was making his way through the deep snow on the pier towards them.

'Is that not young Barry Hall, the grocer's boy?'

'Aye, it kinda looks like him.' Hoynes' eyes narrowed.

Rosy-cheeked and out of breath, the boy reached the side of the *Girl Maggie*. He nodded at the provost out of deference to his office, then turned his attention to Hoynes.

'Mr Hall says he canna get his van doon the quay because of a' this bloody snow.' Young Barry rubbed his nose on his sleeve and snorted deeply.

'Oh right, young fella. In that case, tell him to leave the messages at the weigh hoose and I'll send Hamish up with a handcart tae get them when he appears.'

'Messages? It's a case o' whisky, Mr Hoynes.'

McMurdo, Hoynes and young Barry fell silent for a few seconds. Those who knew the fisherman well would have been able to discern the working of his mind.

'Damn me!' Hoynes shouted in a cloud of exhaled

pipe smoke. 'Auld Hall gets mair deaf by the day. It was only one bottle o' whisky I was after.' He shook his head.

'I'll jeest get him tae take it back then, and I'll bring doon the single bottle,' said Barry, his nose red as Rudolph's.

'No, no, I don't want a young lad like you exerting himself in this weather. No, nor Mr Hall, come tae that. Hamish will sort it oot. Sure, is that not what a first mate is for – eh, Mr McMurdo?'

'Oh, I'm sure. What on earth would you do with a whole case of whisky?' He looked sceptically at Hoynes.

'No, indeed.' Hoynes reached into the pocket of his oilskins. 'Take this for your trouble, lad. It's a penny, but all the change I have aboot me at the moment.' Hoynes flicked the coin through the air, and Barry caught it deftly.

'Thanks very much,' he said, because his mother had brought him up to be polite to his elders. However, the words 'stick the penny up your arse, you miserable auld bugger' were at the very tip of his tongue.

As Hoynes and McMurdo watched the boy wade through the snow back up the pier, they saw two other figures heading towards them.

'At last, my first mate has roused himself fae his bunk and is back in the land of the living. Young folk these days like the hammock, and no mistake.'

'I'll leave you to your day, Sandy,' said McMurdo. 'Nice to see you're applying a lick of paint to impress the newspaper.'

Momentarily Hoynes looked astonished. 'Nothing o' the kind, Mr McMurdo. This is special paint tae help stop the wood fae splitting in the snow. This is a working vessel, no' some exhibition piece.'

'I see.' McMurdo smiled to himself as a large snowflake

landed on the sleeve of his black wool coat. 'My goodness, Sandy, looks like your forecast was wrong!'

'A stray flake or two, nothing more.' He was peering at Hamish and another smaller figure as they struggled through the drifts. 'If that's the reporter Hamish has with him, he's no' a man o' great stature, that's for sure.'

As Provost McMurdo looked over in order to form an opinion, the pair were obscured by a blizzard as the heavy clouds opened over Kinloch.

'I better get back to the town hall while I still can.'

'Aye, maybe for the best,' Hoynes replied, noting with some irritation that the snow had extinguished his pipe.

'You'll hear from the council by five o'clock – you have my word, Sandy.'

'That's good enough for me, Mr McMurdo.'

The provost trudged off through the swirling snow. 'I'm not so sure I'll be coming to you for weather forecasting advice, though.'

As the dark-clad man disappeared into the whiteout, Sandy Hoynes smiled, but the words he muttered under his breath spoke of another expression altogether.

# 6

Though the snow was falling hard, the look of Hamish's companion intrigued Hoynes. Hard to judge the true outline of the man as he was bundled up in a thick jacket and no doubt a stout pullover or two. But to the skipper, even though this Joe was clearly of short stature, his legs looked uncommonly spindly in moleskin trousers. He had a stout toorie pulled down over his face, all but obscuring it. Hoynes wondered as to the nature of his robustness with a difficult passage to Girvan in mind. But the man was a journalist, and surely knew his own limits, he reasoned.

As they met at the side of the *Girl Maggie*, Hoynes held out his gloved hand in order to help the reporter over the gunwale. The hand offered seemed delicate, but thinking of the money, Hoynes cast aside his concerns and helped haul him aboard.

'We better go below!' shouted Hamish as he stepped nimbly from pier to boat like the well-practised mariner he was.

Hoynes nodded in agreement, lifted the hatch, and helped the guest down the short gangway into the cramped quarters below, where bunk beds sat cheek by jowl with a chart table and tiny galley. He pulled out a chair and beckoned to Mr Baird to take no weight at all off his tiny feet.

'You better take off some layers,' he said. 'I'll put them by the stove over there to dry off. I fired it up this morning. It's wee, but as Hamish will tell you, Mr Baird, there's no warmer place than down below on the *Girl Maggie* – even in weather like this.' He looked to his first mate for confirmation, but Hamish was standing in the shadows looking furtive, a nervous smile playing across his lips.

The skipper looked on, smiling proprietorially as the journalist shook the snow free from his overcoat like a dog, and removed his hat and gloves. Hoynes instantly realised why Mr Baird's hand had seemed so delicate.

'Now, I can explain,' said Hamish, holding his right hand before him in a calming gesture.

The briar pipe fell from Hoynes' mouth and landed with a clatter on the galley floor, spilling what was left of its contents, now thankfully extinguished.

Baird held out a hand to Hoynes, who took it, his eyes bulging from his head and mouth flapping like a great cod.

'It's lovely to meet you, Mr Hoynes. Hamish has told me all about you.' From under her neat fringe, Jo Baird smiled broadly. Her face was pale, but her green eyes bore a determined glint.

It was one of these situations whereby had there been room in the cramped crew's quarters Hoynes may have taken his first mate aside for a quiet chat. But as they were all within a few inches of each other, that was impossible.

'Are you feeling unwell, Mr Hoynes?' The journalist looked at the fisherman, her eyes filled with mock concern. 'Or is something else troubling you?'

Hoynes sat back in his chair and finally recovered the power of speech. 'You know, Miss Baird, I've been at the fishing for over fifty years – man and boy – but this is the first time I've had such an experience.'

As Hamish retreated as far away from Hoynes as was physically possible, the journalist looked puzzled. 'And what experience would that be?' She cocked her head, awaiting a reply.

'A woman aboard a fishing boat.'

'Good grief! That's a story in itself, Mr Hoynes. I'm so glad you brought it up.' Miss Baird took a notepad and pen from a bag she'd deposited on the chart table and looked keenly at the skipper. 'Now, can you tell me just why you've never been aboard a fishing boat with a woman?'

'I will. It's well known to be bad luck, the very worst, in fact. Unless you include gentlemen of the cloth, and they all know better.'

'It's nineteen sixty-seven! Have you never heard of women's liberation?'

'Aye, they can be as liberated as they like, but they're no' doing it aboard my vessel. I'll have to ask you to leave, Miss Baird. Snow or no snow!' He turned to Hamish. 'You telt me her name was Joe.'

Before Hamish could speak, the journalist replied for him. 'Hamish was right: my name's Jo, short for Josephine.' She smiled.

'Aye, well, Joe, Davie, Jim – call yourself what you want. I'll no' have women aboard this vessel, and that's an end to it. Only the good Lord knows the brutal fortunes you brought upon us as soon as you set foot on this fine boat. I shouldna be surprised if we're sinking at this very minute.' Hoynes bent down to pick up his pipe.

'Well, I'm afraid I can't do that, Mr Hoynes. You see, you've already taken the newspaper's money, and I'm not willing to go back on the deal.'

'The money's still safe up in the wheelhouse, I'll fetch it for you directly.'

'Oh, the wheelhouse? Is that the tiny thing that looks like half a garden shed?'

'*Half a garden shed!* It's easy seen that you are not acquainted with the rules of the sea, and you know nothing about the vessels that sail upon it.' He shook his big head, jowls wobbling under his white beard. 'I'm heart sorry, for the money was most welcome. But our agreement is over, whether you want it so or not.'

Jo looked at Hamish. 'Will you tell him, or shall I?'

Hamish moved into the light of the storm lantern hanging beside the stove. 'Now, skipper, you'll understand that I had to negotiate in order to get this fine newspaper to feature us. Aye, and it wasn't easy, for as you know, though the *Girl Maggie* might have the best lines of any vessel of the fleet, she's no' the most commodious, and that's just plain-speaking fact.'

'She's the size she is so that she can ride the waves, no' plough through them like some boats I could mention. It's no' all aboot size, Hamish, and well you know it.'

Jo tried hard not to laugh, but she couldn't hide her mirth.

'It's no laughing matter. You didna see they Vikings piling intae great big ships in order to make their way across oceans. The *Girl Maggie* is no different – no different at all.'

'Not quite so sleek,' observed Jo.

'For she has a different function, that's why. If me and Hamish here were set on rape and pillage, well, we'd make sure we had a vessel tae suit. But I'm too auld for such capers, and I'm no' sure Hamish is of that persuasion, even with youth on his side.'

'So you're telling me there's nothing you'd like better than to ravish some poor helpless maidens?' Jo scribbled away with her pen.

'It's jeest an expression, nothing mair. And I've yet to set eyes on a "helpless maiden". There's none tae be found in my hoose at any rate.'

'Nonetheless, you've entered into an agreement, Mr Hoynes, and it's one you'll have to keep.'

'I hand you back the money, and the "agreement" you mention is null and void. It's the rule o' the sea, and no error.'

'Hamish, it's time to come clean.' She looked at the first mate encouragingly.

'Come clean about what, Hamish?' said Hoynes.

Hamish shuffled as much as the space would allow and delved into the pocket of his dungarees. He produced a sheet of paper that had been crumpled rather than folded and handed it to Hoynes.

The skipper reached into his oilskin pocket for his reading glasses. Soon they were perched on his nose as he read the missive in the dim light of the cabin. 'A contract, no less.' He glared at Hamish. 'What right did you have to enter intae any contractual agreement regarding this vessel?'

Hamish's mouth opened, but nothing came out.

'Hamish is your first mate, yes?'

'No' for much longer, he's no'.' said Hoynes, still glaring at his charge.

'Well, as such, he's management, no question about it. As such, his word is binding on a contract regarding the vessel on which he holds this position.' Jo sat back and folded her arms, indicating the end of the discussion.

Hoynes eyed the journalist and his shipmate. He sighed

and removed the glasses from his nose and placed them carefully on the chart table. He looked again at the crumpled document, looked at both of them, and in one swift movement rolled the paper into a ball, placed it in his mouth, and after some chewing and a swig of cold tea from a tin mug before him on the table, winced and swallowed the contract whole. It was his turn to sit back and fold his arms in a gesture of triumph.

'Sandy, you're a hell o' a man,' said Hamish, looking somewhat forlornly at the journalist.

'I'll get you the fiver, and that will be the end o' the matter,' said Hoynes.

'You think?' Jo rummaged through her bag again and produced a manila file. She removed a sheet of paper and waved it in the air. 'This is a signed copy – my copy. And before you think of prising it from my hands in an attempt to consume it, you should note that a third was sent in the post this very morning to the *Glasgow Times*. You're contracted, Mr Hoynes, and that's that!'

'Ha! But you're forgetting that there's no chance the post will be heading up the road today. We're snowbound.' It was Hoynes' turn to smile. 'The postmaster owes me a favour or two. I'll soon get him to find it for me. End of story.'

'You're going to interfere with Her Majesty's Royal Mail? I believe that carries a hefty prison sentence. This story just gets better and better.' Jo scribbled some more.

'Now, jeest hold your horses. I've a duty of care to those aboard my vessel. I'm the captain, after all. In my opinion, the risk of having a wee slip of a lassie aboard on such a perilous journey would be reckless in the extreme.'

'You never read the back of the contract,' said Jo.

'Well, I canna read it now as I've swallowed it.'

'It's a disclaimer – legal and above board. I signed it. You're not responsible for my safety, Mr Hoynes.'

'In that case, I'm jeest no' going to sail, and that's an end to it.'

'Och, Sandy, consider the money. We're to get fifty pounds for our trouble, never mind the fine publicity for us and the toon. We shouldna cut off our noses tae spite oor faces. That's plain daft!' said Hamish.

'Can I have a wee word with you in private, Hamish?' said Hoynes.

The pair made their way back onto the snowy deck; Hoynes, with no little effort, struggling to extract his bulky frame from the tight space.

'Now, listen,' said Hoynes. 'I know fine you were doing what you thought was for the best for me, and for the boat. But I'll no' bring the warth o' bad luck down upon us for taking to sea with a woman. Man, it's bad enough she's aboard while we're tied up at the quay, but we might get away with that on the grounds of a technicality.'

'How so?' said Hamish.

'I brought her aboard in good faith, no' knowing for one instant she was a member of the fairer sex. No, no' even a notion.'

'We'll just have tae sit in port. She's determined, Sandy. She'll likely hold us to oor word for weeks. We'll never fish again.'

'You should keep a lid o'er that glad eye o' yours. She's bonnie enough, or she would be if she had a decent haircut. Maybe a perm like my Maggie.'

'I quite like it. It's all the rage up in Glasgow.'

'That's it, is it? Fair besotted already.' Hoynes rubbed his chin, deep in thought. 'We'll have tae take oor chances. I'm no' green enough behind the ears to know that a contract canna be broken. You take her back to her digs. We'll wait until the agreement is settled later. We should have a manifest of what we've tae pick up in Girvan by this evening. Then we'll dodge off in the middle o' the night. Sit oot at anchor in the sound, if necessary. We'll say that the weather conditions were such that we had to make a bolt for it.'

'Aye, if you're sure we won't end up in the court.'

'We? You signed the damned thing. If anyone's going to court, it'll be you, Hamish.'

Jo popped her head up through the hatch. She looked around and clicked her tongue. 'The weather's worse! Hamish, will you do me a favour, please? I'm not too keen on trudging up the quay and back to the hotel again. Would you mind picking up my stuff? The bill is on account with the paper, so no need to worry about paying. I'm quite cosy here until we sail.' With that, she disappeared back below.

Hoynes looked at his first mate and shook his head. 'We're in a right predicament now, and no mistake. Make yourself useful and away to the weigh hoose. There's a case of whisky from auld Hall sitting in there. And I need a dram!'

'Is it no' a bit early, Sandy?'

'Not a bit of it. It's never too early for a dram when a woman's taken up residence on your own vessel. I'll tell you this: we'll be fair shunned by the rest o' the fleet, and that's a fact. Mind you, it'll no' matter, for something terrible is bound to happen that will make the whole thing academic.'

Hoynes watched as Hamish tramped off up the pier in the scurrying snow.

# 7

After much thought, Sandy Hoynes decided he couldn't, in all conscience, leave his vessel unattended when there was a stray and unwanted female aboard. First, he considered spending the night in his bunk to ensure that this Jo Baird could get up to as little mischief as possible. But the likelihood that this would become a staple of gossip for the people of Kinloch soon dawned on him.

His wife Marjorie was an amiable enough woman. But he feared that she wouldn't take kindly when rumours of his night spent with an attractive young lady were given free flight round the town.

There was only one solution: Hamish must be a nautical chaperone.

'It widna be proper,' said his first mate desperately. 'It would add insult to injury, a single man like me, and a woman – girl – alone all night. In any case, what will my mother say?'

'First of all, it was you who took the notion to sign this damned contract. Not once, mark you, but in triplicate. Secondly, you're too old to be worrying what your mother thinks, fine woman though she is. Heavens, a man has to stand on his own two feet at some point in his life. Have you no' been reading the papers or listening to the wireless? It's the permissive society we're in noo, and no mistake. You could take up with some lassie and take it into your mind tae jump the brush.'

'Get married? There was nothing aboot that in the contract.'

'Now you're being right obdurate. When it comes to nature, there's no' a mair natural thing in the world than a red-blooded man like yourself spending the night wae a well-formed young woman, despite what auld McNee the minister would have you believe. And in any case, it'll be too cold for any carnal urges to take a hold of you.'

'I canna believe I'm hearing this,' said Hamish, sucking hard on his pipe for comfort. 'If your Marjorie could hear you now, she'd be fair dumbstruck, and no error.'

'Well, she'll no' be hearing aboot it.' Hoynes looked up into the dark grey sky. 'I'm going tae drop in at the town hall for terms and the manifest. Then I'm going home for the night. A man of my years canna take any risks in weather like this. And who knows what terror we'll face tomorrow because of your recklessness.'

'And what about Jo?'

'I'll think on that tonight.' Hoynes narrowed his eyes. 'I didna take her for a lassie before she'd her clothes off doon below.'

'No' the most fortunate o' expressions, Sandy, if you don't mind me saying.'

'Och, wheesht, man, I'm thinking. Tell me, does anyone know aboot this bargain you struck?'

Hamish thought for a moment. 'Not that I know of – unless folk in the café were taking notes.'

'You, in your suit, wae a young woman in the café? Don't be daft. The whole toon will be on aboot it.'

'My mother included?'

'Och, she'll be fair raging right at this very moment, I shouldna wonder. But she'll have tae get over it. Man, you're damn near thirty. She canna expect you to remain white as the driven snow for ever.'

'Again, the unfortunate wording, Sandy! And, in any case, how do you know what I've been up tae in my youth?'

'Because you hop from one foot to another like a man wae ants in his breeches every time a lassie so much as hoves intae view.'

Hamish puffed his pipe indignantly.

'No. If I didna recognise her when she was all dubbed up against the snow, you can bet nobody else will. None of the fleet have as keen an eye as me.'

Hamish looked doubtful. 'Aye, maybe you're right. But what aboot all this bad luck you keep banging on aboot?'

'I've been thinking aboot that, as well. When it comes tae matters like this, we have to take intae account the weel of the community. These are extenuating circumstances. Man, the way things are going with this snowfall, the road won't be clear until after Christmas. We have tae balance the good we'll do against the spirits of malevolence. But they're a tricky bunch, they spirits. I'll never forget the Sunday Tommy Meenan cut his toenails.' Hoynes shook his head ruefully.

'What happened?'

'The very next day the lifeboat was oot and hauling the crew aboard before his boat was smashed to pieces on the Barrel Rocks. I was a wean at the time, but I mind my faither put strict rules in place all about the hoose regarding toenail cutting and the like. If you so much as looked at a pair of scissors on a Sunday, you'd have the end o' his belt.'

'Och, you've got me in a right panic, skipper. What on earth am I going to be at with her all night?'

'I'm sure there's a chessboard stowed in the galley. Aye, and Scrabble tae. But you'd be well advised no' to play that with a journalist. She'd likely wipe the floor wae you in a couple o' hands, and you'd be mair miserable than you are right this moment.'

Hamish's face was etched with concern. 'I'll try my best to keep her entertained.'

'And don't let her touch anything!'

'My, Sandy, it's fair personal you are. I've no' thought of such shenanigans!'

'I mean on the boat. You know what they journalists are like, intae everything. You don't want her firing up the engine by mistake, messing wae the compass or something of that nature.'

'I never thought of such a thing.' Hamish looked earnestly at Hoynes. 'Sandy, will you do me one favour?'

'Aye, as long as it doesna involve the lending o' money. You know my opinion o' that caper.'

'No, nothing of the sort! Would you mind giving my mother a call? Jeest to set her mind at ease, you understand.'

'Aye, for who knows what she'll have heard.'

'I know you're the man to put her right, Sandy.'

'I am that.' He pulled on his oilskins. 'Right, I'm off tae see what's going on up at the town hall, then I'm for the fireside and my own bed. Marjorie likely has a right good blaze on the go. Just the ticket. Get some stores in. We canna be too sure how long this voyage intae the unknown will take.'

'Aye, lucky you, toasting your toes in front o' the fire while I'm stuck here wae madam,' said Hamish under his breath. He watched Hoynes struggling through the drifts on the pier until he became a fading yellow ball in the blizzard.

# 8

By his fireside, feet up, Sandy Hoynes worked his way through the manifest of goods to be picked up at Girvan. Though he never trusted the town council, even he had to admit they'd done a good job. Fine deals had been made with traders in Girvan and their counterparts in Kinloch. The fishing boats putting to sea in dangerous weather were to be aptly rewarded. If they all made it back, everyone was a winner. Hoynes lit his pipe in satisfaction.

'You're looking pleased with yourself,' said Marjorie, observing the look on her husband's face.

'Aye, for we'll make a tidy sum, as well as delivering the toon fae the perils o' starvation – and worse, the absence of drink.'

Marjorie raised her eyes. 'As long as you know what you're doing in this weather.'

'It's a straight line tae Girvan! What kind o' mariner would I be if I couldna navigate my way from A to B by just sailing forward?'

'Strange things happen at sea, Sandy. And well you know it.'

Hoynes lifted a crystal glass from the table beside his favourite chair and took a sip of the whisky it held. The phone also occupied this table, and he regarded it with trepidation.

'Why are you staring at the phone?' asked his wife, who missed very little.

'I've a bit o' a dilemma, to tell the truth, Marjorie.'

'Which is?'

'Well, tae cut a long story short, Hamish is babysitting a journalist on board the boat. She's going to cover oor trip tomorrow, for the *Glasgow Times*, no less.'

Marjorie opened her mouth, then closed it again, repeating this action three times before words would come. 'A woman, on the *Girl Maggie*?'

Hoynes waved his hand dismissively. 'Ach, tell me aboot it! She has Hamish under her spell. He signed a contract – in triplicate, mark you. We're done up like a turkey at Christmas. I've no choice other than to honour it.'

Marjorie went back to her knitting, brow furrowed. 'Your own wife and daughter have never set foot on the damned thing, but some lassie fae a newspaper can jump aboard with impunity.'

'I'd no choice. Hamish fair left me in it.'

'Aye, but you're remarkably calm. I'm thinking there's a sum o' money involved.'

Hoynes opted not to reply, as he knew well that his wife would expect a windfall from his payment from the newspaper. He'd give her something, of course, but a sum predicated on a much smaller figure than was the reality.

He reached for the phone and dialled Hamish's phone number.

'Hello, Kinloch 3550, can I help you?'

'Ethel, and how are you keeping?' said Hoynes, as evenly as he could muster. Even he could hear the smile in his voice.

In return there came a scream.

'What on earth's the matter?' Hoynes shot his wife a mystified glance.

'I knew this day would come,' Ethel wailed. 'A deid husband, and a son tae join him!'

'What are you prattling on aboot, woman? Hamish is hale and hearty – well, unless something happened tae him in the short time it took me tae walk from the quay, stop in at the County for a dram, then dive intae the toon hall for some papers.' He thought for a moment. 'Mark you, it did take me a while tae wade through the drifts tae get home. But it's good tae see they've got the miners fae Machrie helping the council boys digging trenches through the snow. Walkways. It reminds me o' my time in the first war.'

He could hear Ethel sigh.

'If I'm not mistaken, you were still at the fishing during the war. A reserved position, I recall.'

Hoynes took a sip of his whisky. 'Aye, you have the right o' it there, Ethel. But I fair kept up wae all that was going on via the newspaper, an' that. You didna have to be at the Front tae experience the fear. And, in any event, I was busy risking my life on the waves tae feed the likes o' you.'

'Aye, out on the sound when it was like a millpond. It was hardly Jason and the Argonauts, Sandy.'

'But yous all tucked into the fish we hauled in! And, anyhow, they Germans were up tae all sorts, what wae the fifth columnists, U-boats and the like. Let me tell you, every day on the sea was like an eternity.' Hoynes heard a muffled snort from Hamish's mother. 'I do have something to report, mind you.'

'I knew it! What have you done to my Hamish? If he's got the jail for the drink, you'll have me tae reckon with! He never touched a drop until he stepped aboard your boat.'

Hoynes frowned at the phone. 'Nothing of the kind! In fact, he's dealing with a damsel in distress.' The wily skipper had considered this problem, and reasoned that making Hamish sound heroic was the most effective way to deal with his mother.

'Well, there's a thing. I would expect nothing less from my son. A right gentleman, so he is. Jeest as I brought him up.'

'Ha! You had him as a raving dipsomaniac a second ago.'

'Sandy Hoynes, you know fine I fear he'll take the same path as his father. I was grateful to you for giving him a berth when – well, when things went wrong. But you must admit yourself, you're no stranger tae a dram, and that's a fact.'

'Hamish can hold his whisky. Aye, and he's not a man of excess neithers.' The memory of Hamish taking a well-lubricated header off the pier at Brodick passed before his mind's eye. But this wasn't the time for such revelations. And, in any case, the tide had been in, and with the help of some sturdy Arran fishermen he'd been hauled out, right as rain.

'Well, I'm glad to hear it. You've no idea how whisky frightens me, Sandy.'

'I've a notion, right enough, Ethel,' said Hoynes, taking another surreptitious sip from his glass. 'But this poor lassie, fair marooned she is, and no' a penny to her name.' Hoynes shook his head sorrowfully, while his wife rolled her eyes. 'No Christian man could turn her away in this weather. I gave her a berth on the boat and promised her passage to Ayrshire tomorrow when we're off to get supplies.'

'I have to say I admire you, Sandy. For it's long before time this nonsense aboot women and boats was put tae rest. We're travelling the world in cruise liners and the like these days. They tell me there was even a female member o' crew on the *Hindenburg*.'

'That's maybe no' the best example, Ethel. But the air and the sea are two very different elements.'

'Well, that's true. But I'm fair glad you had the decency to let me know. I'm no superstitious biddy. It's a fine and noble thing yous are doing. And if any criticism of you or my Hamish reaches my ears, you can rest assured that the appropriate answer will be forthcoming.'

'Aye, and that's right decent o' you, Ethel.' Hoynes hesitated. 'But mark you, there's a wee codicil to this tale.'

'A what?'

'Well, I couldna leave this poor lassie aboard by herself. A fishing boat is fraught wae danger, as you know. Even tied up at the quay.'

'What are you trying tae say, Sandy?'

'Well, jeest that this poor lassie – skin and bones she is, too – I had to gie her a bed for the night, wae a chaperone, you understand.'

'And?' Suspicion was audible in this one word.

'Well, Hamish is making sure she's safe and sound through the night.' Hoynes took the phone from his ear, knowing what was likely to be forthcoming.

He wasn't disappointed.

'You mean my boy is aboard a boat for the whole night – alone! – wae some lassie!'

'Aye.'

'I canna believe it, Sandy. You get doon there right this moment and haul her back onto the quay! If she needs a bed for the night, she can stay here, and Hamish can sleep on the boat. All on his own, as nature intended for a single young man.'

Hoynes grimaced. He'd expected opposition, but not solutions. 'Aye, a noble gesture on your own part, Ethel, yes indeed. But the situation is more complicated than you imagine.'

'I'm no' aboot tae put words to what I'm imagining. What's tae stop this lassie coming up tae the Glebe Fields? I'll have Hamish's bed made up for her in a jiffy. Aye, and I've a fine pot o' broth on the stove, so she'll no' go hungry.'

'She's injured,' said Hoynes, uttering the first thing that came to mind.

'Injured? What kind o' injury?'

'Her leg – it's near snapped in two, so it is.'

'Heavens! The poor girl. But should she no' be in the hospital, rather than a fishing boat?'

'It's the problem o' getting her there. Doctor Duncan came doon earlier wae his Plaster o' Paris and the like. Set it for her exquisitely, if I may say so. Botticelli couldna have done a better job, himself.'

'Is he no' the wee man that has the fish and chip shop at Tarbert?'

'Might be a distant relative, I'm no' right sure. But the dilemma was simple. Wae the roads and pavements fair blocked wae snow, there was no way we could get her up tae the hospital.'

'And how did she get aboard?'

'Aye, that was the tragedy o' the whole thing, Ethel. She slipped on the gunwale as she was coming aboard. Landed wae a right clatter, so she did. That's when the leg got broken.'

'Oh, it jeest gets worse.'

'Aye, it was some performance, right enough. So you'll see, I'm obliged to her in a' sorts o' ways.'

'Could you no' make a sledge and drag her up tae the hospital?'

'I'm a fisherman, Ethel, no' an Eskimo! Anyway, whisky and Eskimos aside, you'll have no fear o' temptation getting the better o' them. The lassie's in agony. I'm sure nature's urging is well beyond her.'

'I'll get my good boots on and head down the pier myself. Hamish can go back hame.'

'Noo jeest hold your horses, Ethel. I've one woman aboard. Another would be tempting fate too far. You must understand my position.' A film of sweat had broken out across his forehead. Hoynes was sure it wasn't the whisky, and the room wasn't overly warm. 'I'm under a lot o' pressure, and that's a fact.'

'You'll be under even mair if nature takes its course. My Hamish is a fine young man – damn near a saint compared to his father. The stirring o' the loins is a force o' nature you canna mess wae.'

'You're havering. Hamish would have to be some monster to take advantage o' a lassie wae her leg in a stookie. When I left them she was fair oot o' it in her bunk. Doctor Duncan gave her a right strong sedative.'

'Well . . .' Ethel still sounded doubtful. 'It would make me much easier o' mind if you were to head down there and sit with the pair o' them. Goodness knows what my Hamish would dae if she took a turn.'

'She'll be fine. But listen, I can hear your concern. I'm just at my tea. I'll head doon the quay just as soon as possible. How does that suit, Ethel?'

Across from him, Marjorie glared.

'Aye, that puts my mind at rest. And you be sure to take care tomorrow. I'll be praying for yous all.'

'Much appreciated, Ethel. And don't worry. There's nobody that knows the way better. Not a skipper in the fleet.'

They said their goodbyes and ended the call.

'My, but you're a piece o' work, Sandy Hoynes,' said Marjorie. 'Still at your tea, indeed! You've been sitting wae a dram for the last hour and more.'

'If I was in France right now they would consider that normal. Drink is all part o' the nourishment o' the body. So, technically I was in the right.'

'Big o' you to go back to the boat, mind you.'

'Ach, I'll be there soon enough. That was a wee white lie. No' even that. I said as soon as possible. In this case, that's tomorrow morning.'

'Sandy Hoynes, one day you'll have tae answer for all the things you've done.'

'Huh, like feeding a starving town? You look to your ain misdemeanours. I've no' forgotten you using packet custard for the tart you put in for the June show and passing it off as your own.'

Marjorie dropped a stitch and rightfully blamed her husband.

# 9

The gull looked out over the loch from his position high on the old fort. Though the waters were as black as pitch, the town gathered around it had a luminous quality, a silvery glow, as though the place was defying night.

A catch of fishermen bustled under the bright lights of the pier. The gull cocked his head to watch as they struggled aboard their vessels, their distant voices, muffled by the snow, floating across the water and up the hill.

The ancient guardian of the town decided to fly over his charges in a spirit of goodwill. The great bird stretched his wings and called out in the still, dark morning. Then, soaring into the velvet sky, he dipped towards the little fleet of fishing boats.

❄

Jim McMichael was sweeping away the accumulated snow from the windows of the *Evening Star*'s wheelhouse. 'Here, Willie,' he shouted to his first mate. 'Is that a new hand Hoynes has aboard? I'm sure I spied someone talking to Hamish when I arrived. By the size o' him, no more than a lad.'

Willie turned his head awkwardly. He'd lost an eye in the

war while serving with the Royal Navy, and wore a patch over the hole where his right one would have been. 'I'm no' quite sure. All I can see is Hoynes himself.'

'Ahoy, *Girl Maggie*!' shouted McMichael. 'You've a new crew member, I see!'

Under the lights of the pier, Hoynes' large, yellow-oilskinned frame was picked out. 'Sorry, my hearing's no' so good these days, Jimmy. What did you say? It's down tae too much exposure to the elements o'er a long period. If you're asking if we'll make it through, I'm sure o' it! Wae the snow being off and suchlike, it'll be plain sailing. Hamish is forecasting clear skies. And, as we all know, he has the sight. Jeest you follow my lead.'

McMichael shook his head and addressed his mate in less strident terms. 'Deaf, my arse. Likely taking advantage o' some schoolboy who's time on his hands. The lad will be getting a pittance for a rough passage and doing all the work. Aye, and Hamish wae the sight, tae – another pile o' pish.'

Before Willie could reply, the call came from the *Girl Maggie*. 'Aye, I heard you. Anyone that sets foot aboard this vessel has the best conditions on the west coast, and that's a fact! And it's been proved time an' again that Hamish is fey.'

'I thought you were deaf!' shouted McMichael.

'Sorry, I didna catch that, Jimmy. I'll need to get going. We've nae time for all this chit-chat.' With that, Hoynes disappeared into his wheelhouse.

Willie arrived by his skipper's side. 'It's funny you said that, Jimmy.'

'How so?'

'Davey fae the *Morning Sky* was having a drink up at the

County wae me last night. Swears that he saw a woman aboard the *Girl Maggie* yesterday. Smoking on the prow, so she was – according tae him, anyway.'

'Don't be ridiculous, Willie! Sandy Hoynes might be up tae many a lark, but even he's no' daft enough tae have a woman aboard. Och, you canna trust a word that comes oot o' Davey's mouth. I'm sure he telt us he'd been tae Buckingham Palace last year.'

'Technically he wisna wrong, Skipper. He was at Buckingham Palace. But it's a pub in Fulham.' Willie shrugged.

'Right, get doon below and fire up the engine. We're going tae be first oot the loch this morning.'

❄

Hoynes squeezed his way through the hatch into the cabin below. Jo was dressed in one of Hamish's thick sea jumpers, black waders and wellington boots, all of which were too large by far. Hamish was attending to some tin mugs beside a simmering kettle. The contrast in temperature was marked, the old potbellied stove doing its job well and heating up the tiny crew quarters.

'You've nae time for tea, Hamish. I'd thought we'd be first away by a long stretch, but McMichael is on the button today. Get the engine fired up and we'll beat them tae it past the island.'

'Oh, can I take some photos?' said Jo.

'You can stay right where you are until we get oot o' the loch and put some sea room between us and the rest o' the fleet. I'll let you know when it's safe to appear.'

'The Dark Ages, right enough,' she murmured to herself.

'Aye, and they'll be staying dark for you until we're in the sound.'

'Aye, aye, captain!' Jo gave a mock salute.

'I'll get the tea, Hamish,' said Hoynes.

'Nae bother. I'll get us going, jeest directly.'

When Hamish disappeared and Hoynes busied himself at the galley, Jo delved into her pocket. In her hand was a little plastic bag with three sugar lumps. She secreted them back into her pocket before Hoynes turned round.

'Do you take sugar?'

'Yes, please, just one spoonful.' She smiled innocently.

'It's lumps we have here. No time for messing aboot wae spoons when a gale's blowing.'

Jo smiled broadly. Being a free spirit, she now viewed the journey as a trip in more ways than one. It was great to be away from the smoke and noise of Glasgow. She was a country girl herself, but from a landlocked part of Stirlingshire. Though boats weren't her thing, she was sure it wouldn't be a problem. After all, she'd performed all sorts of difficult tasks for the paper, including taking photographs at an Old Firm game. No sea could present such dangers.

'Here's your tea,' said Hoynes, handing her a tin mug. 'And in that brown poke there's sugar lumps. You're on tea duties fae now on. We all have tae pull our weight in dire straits like these.'

'Don't worry. I spent my first two years at the paper making tea for those chauvinistic oafs. I'm sure I'll manage.'

'You'll find no chauvinists aboard this vessel. Equality is high on the agenda, and no mistake. Noo, I like my tea sweet – four lumps. When I call doon fae the wheelhouse, you get yourself moving quick smart, lassie.'

Jo raised her brows.

Suddenly the boat shuddered as the Gardner engine thudded into life. After a few coughs and splutters, it soon settled into a steady pulse, like an old man struggling out of bed in the morning, coughing, cursing and then hurrying off to the toilet.

'Aye, there's a fine sound, right enough. Next stop, Girvan. I better go and get us underway. You mind and stay here until I give you a shout.'

Hoynes climbed through the hatch and onto the deck, just as Hamish emerged from the engine. The skipper cast his eye about and noticed that McMichael was about to sail; first mate Willie was busy at a hawser looped over a bollard on the quayside.

'Quick, Hamish, get you up on that quay and untie us! McMichael's making a break for it. Mind, we've got the press aboard – even though she's just a slip o' a thing – and we don't want the vessel portrayed as some sluggard in a national paper. It widna be good for morale at all.'

'Whose morale?' Hamish asked.

'Mine. Noo, get a shift on.'

Hamish strode across the snowbound deck, and in one fluid movement hurdled up onto the pier. As he busied himself untying the vessel, Hoynes squeezed into the small wheelhouse and began the manoeuvre away from the quay, his eyes flicking between the loch ahead and the progress of the *Morning Star*.

Job done, Hamish leapt back aboard in his usual manner, forgetting about the snow. Luckily, he skidded into a mess of nets, only his dignity hurt.

'Serve you right!' shouted Hoynes. 'There's nae place for a' that flash stuff on a serious vessel like this.'

'It was you that wanted away quickly! The way you were turning, it would jeest have been you and Jo as a crew, for I'd have been left on the pier like a right dumpling.'

'Wheesht! I'm concentrating, man.' The tip of Hoynes' tongue was sticking out between his teeth as he made for the open water of the loch with all speed, well aware that – as things stood – he was on a collision course with the *Evening Star*.

'You're going tae see us wrecked before we even make harbour!' shouted Hamish. 'How will that look in the newspaper?'

The two fishing boats were neck and neck now. Hoynes looked to his left, only to see McMichael signalling to him with his right hand in a way that could best be described as ungentlemanly.

The *Evening Star* was a bigger boat, of more recent manufacture, but with size came a sluggishness of acceleration. Though McMichael had been first to leave the quayside, Hoynes was gaining on him as they both made for the gap between the twin piers.

'You'll need tae get a move on, Sandy!' yelled Hamish, as black smoke issued in great clouds from the wheelhouse chimney.

'I know what I'm at, Hamish.' Hoynes returned McMichael's crude gesture with gusto.

'We needna worry about beating them to the loch, Sandy. Once we're in open water, we'll gain on them.'

'I'm in command here. And we'll be first oot o' this harbour. I'll bet my life on it!'

❄

A collection of elderly fishermen had gathered on the quayside. Ostensibly they were there to wish their former colleagues godspeed, but also with an eye to any calamities or notable happenings that they could discuss over a dram later.

'Bugger me,' said Peeny. 'It's like watching two slugs racing for a plughole.'

'McMichael is a determined bugger, right enough,' said McKirdy. 'But Sandy Hoynes should know better. Whoot's the point in sinking two boats jeest tae see who can make it oot the harbour first? Aye, wae whisky supplies aboot tae run low in the whole community.'

'By the look o' that smoke piling fae the *Girl Maggie* they'll no' make it to the end of the pier, never mind Girvan,' observed Peeny.

By this time, the spectators included the crews of the other boats in the fleet. Their heads appeared through portholes, above hatches and through wheelhouse windows, as the race progressed slowly, but with no little excitement.

'McMichael's got the better o' it, and no mistake,' said Peeny. 'Hoynes is bound tae end up wae egg on his face.'

'There's been bad blood between the pair o' them since that darts match at the Douglas Arms,' said Tommy Duncan, his pyjama collar poking out the neck of his pea jacket. 'If you recall, Sandy had tae score twenty-one off three darts. Mind, he missed the board and near blinded auld Jenny. McMichael cleaned up. They County boys took it right bad, so they did.'

Both fishing boats were now nearing the gap between the two piers, the *Evening Star* ahead by a nose. Those on the quay and on the remaining boats considered the race was won – until something extraordinary happened.

A head appeared from the cabin hatch of the *Girl Maggie*. McMichael was the first to spot it, and sheer shock caused him to let go of the wheel. His boat veered dangerously to the right, heading for the new quay on the other side of the harbour.

Hoynes saw his chance, cut in ahead of his rival and made it out into the open loch first. He had the time to return McMichael's earlier gesture again as he coasted past the *Evening Star*, her skipper desperately turning the wheel to avoid a collision.

The faces of those back at the quay, fishermen young and old, bore a collective look of disbelief.

'I must have had too much tae drink last night, for I could swear I jeest saw a lassie poke her heid oot o' Sandy's hatch thonder.'

'Well, I never touched a drop,' said Duncan, 'and I saw her too.'

Provost McMurdo and the town clerk appeared. 'Oh, we've missed the first boys away,' said the former, slightly bemused by the stricken looks on the faces of those before him. 'Is there something wrong?'

Peeny turned to the provost. 'Hoynes has a woman – a lassie! – aboard his boat. We all saw her.'

'Oh, well, I can't see that being a problem,' replied the provost.

The old fisherman fixed him with a steely glare. 'You're a vet tae trade, Mr McMurdo, yes?'

'Yes, what about it?'

'Well, think on. A fisherman going tae sea with a woman aboard a boat is as vexatious as a vet leaving his wallet in a barn. Do you get my point?'

'Oh dear.'

'Aye, oh dear indeed! It doesna do tae provoke the traditions of the sea – no, not at all. I'll be surprised if we set eyes on Sandy Hoynes and his boat again, and that's a fact.'

With a general murmur of agreement, those gathered on the quay shuffled off, heads down, as though they were stepping away in widow's weeds from a funeral.

# 10

The *Girl Maggie* forged ahead in the still waters of the loch, easily beating her rival between the two buoys that marked the channel past the island and into the sound.

When Hoynes glanced behind, the first grey light of day revealed a ragged string of fishing boats in his wake, headed by the *Evening Star*. He smiled at the thought of his fellow skipper's indignation over losing the impromptu race out of the harbour. But he was puzzled as to why McMichael had made such an elementary mistake in steering. In any event, Kinloch's fishing fleet had set sail to rescue the town from starvation. He was merely first amongst equals. He smiled at the thought. As he turned to face forwards, a large gull deposited a great mess across the wheelhouse window.

'Here, get that cleaned off, Hamish!' shouted Hoynes. 'These bloody gulls.'

In short order, Hamish appeared in front of the window and went to work with a chamois leather and bucket of soapy water, his breath clouding in front of him.

Hoynes popped his head out of the wheelhouse door and looked heavenward. Now that the first light of dawn was spreading across the eastern horizon, it revealed a great bank of cloud ahead, dark but with the pearlescent quality of snow. Though he could see the Isle of Arran to his left, the Ayrshire coast – their destination – had not emerged with the dawn.

'Your predictions are awry again, Hamish. I'm thinking you should stay clear o' weather forecasting, for that cloud is just about to dump a great blizzard upon us.'

Sure enough, as he spoke, the first flakes appeared on Hamish's Breton cap.

'And jeest where did you get that fancy bunnet?' Hoynes asked. 'You look like one o' they French matelots, no' a proper Scots fisherman.'

'Och, they're a' the rage in London. I'm sure they Beatles were wearing them no' that long ago.'

'Well, if that's no' enough to put you off such millinery, I don't know what is. There's nae room for a fashion statement aboard a vessel o' the sea. The minute you pick up the guitar, you're back ashore, and no mistake.'

Gradually, as though the emergence of the day had been merely a short respite, darkness engulfed the *Girl Maggie*. Not the pitch black of night, but an eerie grey that rendered their surroundings almost invisible. Even the water lapping at the sides of the vessel was muffled, as though they had put to sea in a small pond. Great clouds of snow began to sweep over the fishing boat.

Hamish joined Hoynes in the wheelhouse. 'My goodness, skipper. I don't think I've ever put to sea in conditions like this. It's as though we've entered another realm.'

'You have a flair for the dramatic, Hamish. Och, you get that from your mother. The hoops I'd tae go through tae stop her from heading doon the quay last night to save your virtue near turned me into a circus dog. It's time you put your foot doon and showed her who's boss. You canna go on at the beck an' call o' your mother, no' a man your age.'

'It's a' very well saying that, Sandy. But where would I go? I can rustle up some beans and bacon, but that's aboot it. And when it comes tae a' this washing and pressing o' clothes – well, that's me buggered.'

'It's a wife you're needing, plain and simple. Nature is designed wae that in mind. While we're oot braving the wild ocean, they're at home attending tae the tasks that are a mystery tae menfolk. I have these twin tubs in the kitchen now. Man, they might as well be fae outer space, for I've no idea how to use them. But Marjorie fair swings intae action. Before you know it, the scullery is filled wae steam and she's hauling wet clothes hither and thon. Quite miraculous it is tae watch.'

'My auld mother still has a mangle. She's got forearms like a miner, so she has.'

Hoynes lit his pipe thoughtfully. In truth, he'd always felt rather inferior to the opposite sex. The manner in which they dealt with everything from domestic tasks to wiping the backsides of infants had to be admired. He'd been forced to change his daughter's nappy on mercifully few occasions. Each time it had ruined his appetite for days, and the mere sight of oxtail soup set his stomach churning to this day. But Marjorie performed the task with alacrity, happily conversing as she dealt with a great deposit the size of which a carthorse would have been proud.

'You wait, Hamish. Wae this women's lib and all, there will be a woman sitting in Downing Street before you can canter.'

'Och, no.' Hamish removed his cap and slicked back his diminishing quiff with an oily hand. 'It widna be proper.'

'What do you have tae say aboot Her Majesty, in that case? Would you no' consider that she's making a fair fist o' things?'

'Aye, but she's got the royal blood, Sandy. Look at auld Victoria, for example. She was only a slip o' a lassie when she became queen and she ruled a huge empire. I'm sure your Marjorie couldna set her hands tae that. No offence, mark you.'

'Maybe no', but I think your mother would give it a go.'

Hamish nodded, a faraway look in his eyes. 'You might be right there.'

'There's a condition wae women who've lost their husbands in tragic circumstances and the like.'

'And jeest what would that be?' Hamish asked.

'Och, they become fair attached tae their sons. No' in any romantic way, you understand, but enough that they want them aboot the place. Put it like this, have you ever brought home a lassie that met with your mother's approval?'

'That's a simple question tae answer, skipper. I've never brought a lassie hame at all. My mother would just find fault.'

'Aye, an' you were close enough wae Jessie McGown for a good while.'

'I was.' Hamish lowered his head.

'You never told me why it all came tae an end.'

A look of regret passed over the first mate's face. 'My mother wisna keen. Apparently Jessie's great-grandfather had been hung by the Duke o' Argyll for poaching. You canna bring blood like that intae the family line.'

'Nonsense. I knew the man. I was only a boy, but I can see him yet. He was a shepherd doon at Pollyfergus farm in Blaan. A fine fellow. Died on the hill wae his sheep, as all men o' that trade are want tae do.'

Hamish looked momentarily bewildered. 'Are you sure?'

'I am that. Sure, he was great pals wae my own grandfaither. He was a man o' the land. On my mother's side, you understand.'

'So my mother didna have the right o' it at all?'

'No. And I'm here tae tell you that she knew fine what she was at. Jeest fair keen that you stayed by her fireside.'

'I can hardly believe it.'

'I'm telling you, Hamish. You need tae get yourself sorted wae a nice lassie, quick smart. I know you're proud o' thon coo's lick o' yours. But, man, that'll no' last for ever. And once you're bald, you've nae chance finding a wife.'

'In that event I'll jeest keep my bunnet on, Sandy.'

'Ach, you're havering. You'll pardon me for the descriptive nature of what I'm aboot tae say. You'd be a bonny sight, fair caught up in the throes o' passion in your marriage bed, and you wae your bunnet on. Man, you might as well have your pipe clenched between your teeth intae the bargain.'

It was hard to gauge what Hamish thought of this. His expression went from one of abject horror to an embarrassed red hue. Almost as though the mere contemplation of the carnal act minus pipe and bunnet may well be a sin against all that was holy.

The snow was now falling like feathers from a burst pillow. 'I hope my calculations are right,' said Hoynes, 'or we'll fair batter intae the Cock o' Arran. For I don't know aboot you, but I canna see much beyond the prow.'

'I'm getting a bad feeling, Sandy.'

'Again? My, but you're a right doom-monger. You'll need tae brighten up your act. No woman wants to be wed tae some prophet o' doom.' With that, Hoynes sounded the ship's horn in the unlikely event that some other vessel was in the vicinity. For it had to be said, only the bravest or most foolish of mariners would have put to sea this day. Though it all depended on your perspective.

# 11

Down below, things on the *Girl Maggie* had taken a turn for the worse, as far as Jo was concerned. She'd stuck her head above the cabin hatch for just a moment as they were leaving the harbour. But even in those calm waters, just a glimpse of the houses on the north shore of the loch swaying to and fro was enough to set her stomach churning.

She'd consulted the large stained chart that sat before her on the table. Though she knew next to nothing about the ways of the sea, she calculated that the alarming change in circumstances aboard coincided with their emergence into the sound. It was plain enough on the chart.

The *Girl Maggie* lurched in the swell, and with it the journalist's stomach. She tried to focus on a little copper cooking pot that hung from a nail over the stove, reasoning that orientating herself within the cabin may ease her plight. But this had the opposite effect, and she felt the bile rise in her throat. Thankfully, there was an old bucket close at hand, into which she vomited copiously.

Believing that her symptoms would now ease, she rested her head on the chart table. Unfortunately, this only made matters worse, and in a few moments she was retching again into the bucket.

She remembered a story she'd read about Admiral Lord Nelson. As a young midshipman he'd suffered terrible seasickness, making his first three years or so aboard a man-of-war hell. Miserably, Jo tried to console herself that this was a relatively short journey, or so Hoynes had assured her.

Hamish stuck his head through the hatch, his Breton cap defying gravity and remaining attached firmly to his head. 'How are you faring down below?' he asked.

Through her misery, Jo managed a retort. 'That's a very personal question to ask a young lady.'

Hamish looked startled. 'Och, I meant . . . I meant no offence. Jeest wondered how you were managing, and the like,' he stammered, face bright red.

'It wouldn't be polite to give a truthful answer.' Again Jo bent over the bucket.

'Oh dear!' Hamish eased his way through the hatch and into the cabin. 'It'll be the seasickness you have.'

'I kinda worked that out for myself.'

'Och, not tae worry. There's barely a man – or woman – at sea who takes to it right away. Though, mark you, they say they do. I myself was right seasick when I first landed aboard a vessel. But it soon passed.'

'How long did it take?' Jo asked quickly before heaving again.

'No time at all. Less than a year, at any rate.'

'Let me die now,' she groaned, laying her head back on the chart table.

'I know fine what you require: a nice mug o' tea. My mother swears by it, a cure-all suitable for every occasion. Personally, I prefer a dram myself, but I do believe women are of a different construction.'

'So you've just noticed?'

Ignoring the barb, Hamish set to and hung the iron kettle above the stove. 'I'll make you a brew.'

As her head lolled from side to side on the chart table, the thought of a cup of tea only made Jo feel worse.

Then she had an idea. 'Thank you, Hamish. I'd love some tea, please.'

'It'll set your stomach to rights in no time.'

But just as he was preparing three tin mugs, a loud voice sounded through the speaking tube from the wheelhouse above.

'Get your backside up here, Hamish. I canna see a thing. We'll have tae take it slow and check depths.'

'I'll need to go back on deck. My goodness, that's a call dreaded aboard any vessel. It usually only happens in the worst fog. But this snow has the same effect. I'll be back down directly and make you some tea. But colliding wae the Cock o' Arran would do us no favours at all.'

'The cock of who?' said Jo groggily.

'Never you mind.'

As his wellington boots disappeared through the hatch, Jo's heart sank. The prospect of a mug of tea had suddenly become an attractive one, but not perhaps for the reasons Hamish assumed. She laid her head back on the table and tried to will herself not to be sick again.

❄

Hamish whirled the line with the brass end through the air, as though he was about to lasso a horse. At exactly the right moment he let it go, and just like a cast from an expert fly fisherman it disappeared through the heavy snow and landed well to the port side of the *Girl Maggie* with a thick plop in the unseen swell.

It was eerie, with not a seabird to be heard, or sight of land or sky. The deck of the boat was now garnished with a thick icing of snow. Hoynes peered out from the wheelhouse through a window frosted like a shop from a Dickensian Christmas scene. 'How's she looking?' he shouted to Hamish as he hauled in the line.

'Aye, we're okay, Sandy. We'll have to take it steady, mind. When did you get your last bearing?'

'Jeest after we passed the island, Hamish. I'm pretty sure we're on course, but cocooned like this it's hard to tell if it's New Year or New York!'

'I'll fling the line every few minutes, just to make sure.'

'Aye, we'll come across the seabed long before we hit the rocks. But I'm convinced we're on the mark, tae. Mind you, I'll take her down to a crawl, jeest in case.' The tone of the engine lowered as the skipper slowed the craft.

'It's jeest like being Jonah – you know, stuck in the belly o' the whale,' said Hamish.

'Damn me, it wisna snowing in there tae, was it?'

'I'm wondering. Would it no' be safer to turn roon and go back the way we came? You surely weren't expecting a blizzard like this when we set off, Sandy?'

'I listened to two sources of information: the shipping forecast and your predictions. It would appear that both were sadly lacking. As far as turning round, what good would that do us? We could go clattering intae the rest o' the fleet. I don't want to be the man responsible for scuppering this emergency mission.'

Hamish nodded sagely at this reasoning.

'I'm like a block o' ice, Hamish. You take the wheel a while. Keep her on the current heading unless you have a notion we're nearing the rocks. I'll away and warm my backside at the stove and get a mug o' tea. How's the lassie doing, by the way?'

'Och, no' good at all, Sandy. She's seasick.'

'You canna expect much else fae a lassie. It'll teach her tae be so forthcoming and manipulative in order tae get aboard this vessel in the first place. Right cunning, if ever I saw it.'

'Will you get her a mug, skipper? I was about to when you asked me to haul the line.'

'Hopefully that will brighten her up. There's nothing like tea for altering your outlook on life – aside fae a dram, that is. It's no' quite the time tae splice the main brace yet.' He squinted at the sky. 'Though that time might come before we get back hame.'

Hoynes left the wheelhouse, to be replaced by Hamish. The skipper held out his gloved hand and almost immediately it gathered a covering of snow. He shook his head and made for the hatch.

# 12

Jo had managed to make it to the stove. She'd set herself a mug and poured some water into the tin teapot, to which Hamish had already added some tea leaves. She reached into her pocket and found the small packet containing the sugar lumps. She'd have been tempted to forgo the tea and just dissolve one on her tongue, but the thought of it made her stomach churn. She was also bitterly cold, so the warm beverage would be most welcome.

Jo was just about to place the sugar lump in her mug when Hoynes burst through the hatch like a cork fired from a gun. He landed on his feet with a thud, hard enough that he had to bend his knees in order to absorb the impact. Startled, Jo dropped the sugar lump not in her mug, but in the open packet used by the crew.

Hoynes eyed the hatch with disdain. 'Man, I'll need tae get that widened. The wood has fair contracted over the years. It's the effects of salt water, you understand.'

Though the cognitive part of Jo's brain registered this as nonsense, and it was obvious that, on the contrary, Sandy Hoynes' waistline had burgeoned, she didn't have the energy to contradict him. She slumped at the side of the galley, the cabin spinning as though she was on a merry-go-round.

'Here now, this won't do, no, not all.' He caught her under the arms and hefted the seasick journalist into the bottom bunk, normally reserved for his own use. 'Why don't you have a wee lie doon and I'll fetch you some tea. This isn't quite the jolly you imagined it would be, eh?'

Jo now felt so miserable she could barely muster a reply. She grunted and turned over on her side to see if it would banish her nausea.

Hoynes made for the galley, the curtain that separated it from the rest of the cabin already pulled aside. He placed the kettle back on the hook and soon heard it bubble to the boil. He prepared two mugs, noticing that the young journalist had already laid one out for herself. 'How many sugars?' he asked her.

'Just one, please,' she replied weakly.

'This will sort you out. If it doesna, the only place for you is up on deck. You need tae catch sight o' the horizon. Mind you, right at the moment there's no horizon tae be seen.' He reached for the sugar and put four lumps in his own mug, then two for Hamish and one for his stricken passenger. Hoynes stirred the leaves in the tin pot sitting snugly in its little guard nest on the stove.

As he waited for the tea to brew, he reached for the speaking tube. 'How are we looking, Hamish?'

'So far, so good,' came the muffled reply from the wheelhouse. 'But if anything, the snow's heavier than it was just a couple o' minutes ago when you went below.'

He shook his head. 'I've never seen the like. I'll give you a shout when the tea's brewed. I'll hand it up through the hatch.'

Satisfied that the brew was sufficiently infused, Hoynes poured the tea into each mug. The sound of tea pouring was always a comfort, the ritual of making it almost as satisfying as the beverage itself. He gave each mug a stir, added some milk from the bottle kept in an ice bucket he'd purloined from the County Hotel, and took a sip from his own mug to make sure all was well.

He tapped Jo on the shoulder. 'Here, get this doon you, lassie. I hope the next time you're sitting in your fancy office in Glasgow you'll take note o' the desperate conditions us fishermen have to endure. Man o' man, the whole profession is fair heroic, and no mistake.'

She turned round in the bunk and accepted the mug of tea with trembling hands.

'I canna see you being in any condition to take photographs and write your piece. Wae this snow, there's no' so much tae photograph at the moment.' He took a sip of his tea thoughtfully. 'Would you like me tae jot down a few o' my musings? Jeest tae give you a hand, what wae you in your current plight an' all.'

'I don't mind,' replied Jo wearily. 'I just want to feel better again.'

'And you will, you will. I better get Hamish his tea. He's a right bugger if it gets cold. Fair pampered by that mother o' his.' Hoynes had another thought. 'You're a single lassie yourself, are you not?'

'What? Oh, yes.'

'Aye, well, you could do worse than a fisherman. Oor Hamish is a fine man. Good family – well, apart from his faither, and that was a weakness for the bottle, nothing mair.'

Jo ignored Hoynes' attempts at matchmaking. The thought of becoming romantically involved with the man in the ancient suit, receding hairline and weird eyes was enough to send her stomach churning again. 'Could you please pass me that bucket?'

Hoynes pushed the bucket across the cabin with the toe of his sea boot. 'I see it's no' your first visit tae it, neither.' He gave Hamish a shout through the speaking tube. His first mate came to the hatch and took the two mugs of tea handed to him.

As Hoynes began his squeeze through the hatch back to the deck, he heard Jo mumble. 'What's that, lassie?' Hoynes leaned his head back into the cabin.

'Don't drink the tea.' Her voice was slurred now. Plainly she was suffering.

'Don't you worry. Jeest you concentrate on getting better.'

With that, he was back on the snowy deck.

Hoynes gave the wheelhouse window another rub before joining Hamish in the cramped space. The blizzard was so heavy now that it was hard to see the bow of the *Girl Maggie*. The skipper sipped his hot tea thoughtfully.

'This isna the kind o' trip we envisaged, skipper. No, not at all,' said Hamish as he peered into the snow, ship's wheel in his brawny hands.

'No. I wished we'd jeest turned doon the offer. Though it would've been a miserable time for the folk in Kinloch if we hadn't volunteered. I daresay a few would have resorted tae cannibalism when the food became scarce.'

'I know just who, tae.' Hamish shook his head.

'We can only pray that things improve.'

'Aye, you're right there.'

# 13

On board the *Evening Star*, McMichael was becoming increasingly concerned by the turn of the weather. Unlike Hoynes – who thought such a thing an unnecessary indulgence, not to mention an unthinkable expense – he had a radio.

'*Evening Star* to the Kinloch fleet, come in, over.' He waited for a few moments, but there was nothing but static on the crackling line. McMichael was about to give up when a faint voice sounded through the wooden speaker above his head. 'Aye, Jim, it's Davie here.'

'Davie who?'

'Davie Robertson, who do you think?'

'You're supposed tae say, "Roger, the *Black Isle* receiving, over."'

'Och, I canna get tae grips wae this radio stuff at all. You knew fine who it was as soon as I opened my mouth. You only saw me this morning.'

'That's no' the point. We should be observing the correct protocol on the wireless. You never know who's listening.'

'It's hardly Radio Caroline, Jim.'

'Clyde Coastguard, they'll have their lugs roon this, and no mistake.'

'You're worried about who's listening to your radio protocol when we're out here about tae crash intae Arran in a blizzard. You're a brave man, right enough, McMichael, but I'm no' so sure about your priorities.'

'It's why we're speaking! I think we should turn roon and make back for Kinloch.'

Apart from the crackle of static, there was silence on the other end of the line. 'Davie, are you there?'

'You're supposed tae say, "Come in, *Black Isle*"!'

'Well, what dae you think?'

'Roger. I've been conversing wae the crew, and we're o' the same mind as yourself, over.'

'And you're certain sure, Davie?'

'I'm in no hurry tae land on the Cock o' Arran. We'll make oor way back hame. I'll pass it doon the fleet.'

'What about Hoynes?'

'No' even a radio on board, has he?'

'No, nor a glimmer o' one. The man's too tight.'

'It's for the good o' the many. He'll have tae take his chances. In this, who knows if any of us will make it back.'

'Aye, you're right. I'll try and get the Coastguard and tell them he's out there somewhere.' McMichael squinted into the gloom. He'd never been the best of friends with Sandy Hoynes – the man was overbearing at the best of times; still, he wished him no harm. He lifted the radio to his mouth again and called Clyde Coastguard.

❄

Hoynes enjoyed his mug of tea. A great wave of warmth had spread into his belly. And now, despite the weather, he found himself quite relaxed in the wheelhouse.

Idly, he watched Hamish swirl the line yet again. The whole process became strangely fascinating. The brass end seemed to be drawing shapes in the snowy sky. At first they were random, then he began to notice more discernible patterns.

'You're the clever one wae that line, Hamish,' he said to his first mate. 'I'm sure I can see my grandmother.'

'You can what?'

Hamish let the line go, and Hoynes watched it arc away until it disappeared into the blizzard. He rubbed his eyes. It was as though a rainbow had appeared where the line had landed. It was a tiny rainbow, but a rainbow nonetheless.

'Well, in all my days, I've never seen the like. Have you, Hamish?'

'No, this snow's as thick as she comes.'

'No, the rainbow, Hamish. You've got to say, that's a phenomenon, if ever there was such a thing.'

Hamish said nothing as he hauled at the rope, thinking that Hoynes was having him on. It wouldn't be the first time the wily old skipper had set him up for some prank or other.

Hoynes gasped as Hamish pulled the line back over the side. 'Now, what's the chances o' that, eh?'

'Of what?' said Hamish, still unwilling to be taken in.

'I've never seen it done before, man o' man! It's the biggest lobster I've ever set eyes on, and no mistake. Here, I'll help you get they claws under control. A thing that bloody size could have your heid off, Hamish.' Hoynes was framed in the door of the wheelhouse with a heavy spanner.

'Right, what's the joke? Are you sure this is the right time to be messing aboot, skipper?'

'It'll be no joke when that lobster has you in its clutches. You stand still, and I'll whack it wae this.' Hoynes edged towards Hamish on tiptoes across the snowy deck, the spanner clasped in his right fist.

'You're going to dae yourself a mischief. Whatever you're playing at, well, it's no' funny!' Hamish edged away from Hoynes.

Without warning, Hoynes lunged forward, brandishing the spanner. Briefly he flew through the air until both he and the spanner landed with a crash on the deck. Thankfully, the deep snow broke his fall, though he cursed as he struggled on the deck.

'What on earth are you at, Sandy? You damn near broke your neck.'

Hoynes staggered back to his feet, seemingly no worse for his leap through the air. He looked about anxiously, as though he was frightened something would come out of the shifting curtains of snow and do him harm. 'Would you believe it? How on earth did the big bugger get up there?'

'What big bugger?'

'The bloody lobster! It's taken a fair jump tae get on top o' the wheelhouse.' He took off his bunnet and scratched his head for a moment. 'Come tae think o' it, I've never seen such a creature jump. Have you, Hamish?'

'Sandy, you're starting tae worry me.' Hamish bit his lip. 'I've heard o' people seeing strange apparitions in the desert. Hallucinating water and palm trees where there's none at all.'

Hoynes looked at him in disbelief. 'You might no' have noticed, but we're most certainly not in the desert. This is a blizzard, Hamish!'

The first mate sighed with relief. 'Och, you've been winding me up, Sandy. You had me worried for a while, there.'

'Ach, you're never done worrying. You check the line while

I work out what we'll do.'

'I will. So you're still of a mind tae turn back, skipper?'

'Not in the slightest!'

Hamish looked confused. 'Well, what are you planning to do?'

'I'm going tae get that huge bloody lobster doon off that wheelhouse, that's what I'm going to do.'

'Now, wait a minute, Sandy. I'm concerned, and that's for sure. What did you have for your tea last night? It wisna shellfish, by any chance? A bad clam or a mussel can fair set a man's heid awry.'

Hoynes was now studying the wheelhouse like a mountaineer might Ben Nevis. 'You'll need tae gie me a hunker up, Hamish. Better still, get doon below and grab that set o' ladders. I'll catch the bugger yet!'

'Get back in and steer the boat, Sandy. Less o' the messing about!'

'Aye, good idea. I'll keep us on the straight and narrow while you get they steps.' He entered the wheelhouse. 'Man, you should hear the racket the damn thing's making on this roof. Mind, it'll fetch a pretty penny.'

Hamish hesitated, then darted down the hatch to the cabin below.

# 14

Hamish stood by the stove in the small cabin wringing his hands. He'd seen his skipper drunk on many occasions. At such times, he was prone to bouts of immodesty, and could even become argumentative. But Hamish had never known him to have hallucinations. And, in any case, Hoynes hadn't touched a drop.

'What's up with you?' said Jo, stirring in the bunk and giving Hamish a fright. In his puzzlement about Hoynes, he'd forgotten all about the reporter.

'The skipper's behaving in a very strange fashion. I canna fathom it at all.'

'What's he doing?'

'Och, I won't burden you with it, you being so seasick and all.'

Jo looked wary. 'I'm feeling a bit better, actually. The lie down must have done me some good.' She looked at Hamish from the corner of her eye. 'Just what do you mean by "behaving in a very strange fashion"?'

'He's no' himself, that's all.'

'If you don't mind me saying, he seemed a bit odd to me from the start.'

'In what way?'

'A wee bit eccentric, perhaps?'

'Not at all, he's the most practical man I know.'

'So what's changed?'

'If I tell you, you've got tae promise you won't put it in the paper.'

'Don't be daft.' Though she was trying to sound upbeat, Jo felt her heart sink. Suddenly, her seasickness was the last thing on her mind.

'Well . . .' began Hamish hesitantly, 'he's seeing things.'

'Oh, what kind of things?'

'Tae put it plainly, he thinks there's a giant lobster atop the wheelhouse.' Hamish looked at Jo with a desperate look etched across his face.

'I see.' She bit her lip.

'You don't look very surprised. I can assure you, this is far from the normal turn o' events on a vessel like this. I'm worried he could be ill. My granny had a stroke and didna know who anybody was, even her own daughter.' He thought for a moment. 'Well, apart fae auld Joe Kennedy the undertaker, but apparently they'd been close years before. You can imagine how upset my poor mother felt.'

'Right.' Jo was sitting up now, biting her lip. 'Hamish, I have a confession to make.'

'For all that's holy, you're no' seeing things as well, are you?'

'No, but I think I know what's wrong with Mr Hoynes.'

'You dae?'

'You'll have heard of LSD, Hamish.'

'Pounds, shillings and pence? Of course I've heard of it. I'm no' some daftie!'

'I mean the other LSD. You know – drugs. I assume that

Kinloch isn't so isolated that some notion of the swinging sixties hasn't reached the place.'

Hamish looked alarmed. 'You mean like they Trolling Stones? No, Sandy widna have any truck wae that carry-on. In any case, Marjorie would make his life a misery if he was at such nonsense.'

'No, you're not getting this. Let me explain.' Jo went on to tell the distressed mariner just how a sugar lump impregnated with LSD had landed in Hoynes' mug of tea.

It took Hamish a while to digest this information. He stood with his mouth open for a while, making to speak, but not quite managing it. Eventually he found his voice. 'And jeest how long does this last, this LSD?'

Jo shrugged. 'It's hard to tell. Everyone reacts differently. It's really interesting, sets your mind free.'

'I'm quite happy wae my mind staying exactly where it is, thank you. I canna see any joy in conjuring up images of giant shellfish, or the like. What have you done?'

'It's okay, calm down.' Jo made to lift herself out of the bunk, but a wave of nausea swept over her and she was forced to fall back on the old blankets.

'Calm? How can any soul stay calm in these circumstances? We're lost in a blizzard at sea, and the skipper's turned intae a cabbage!'

'But you can steer the boat, yes?'

'Oh aye, I can steer the boat under normal circumstances. We call it navigation in the trade. But these are no' normal circumstances, no' by a long chalk. I've never sailed in such weather conditions.'

'Oh, come on, Hamish! Where's your confidence? It's time to step up, show what you're made of.'

'I'll tell you where my confidence is, up on top o' the wheelhouse wae that great lobster. Sandy plays the fool fae time tae time, o' that there's no doubt. But there's no' a finer sailor on the west coast.'

'Go up and see what's happening. It shouldn't be too hard to reason with him. Folk are usually quite placid under the influence.'

'I widna say he was placid. No' by a long shot. He's determined tae beat the brains oot o' this poor lobster. I mean, he's no' normally a cruel man.'

'For a start, Hamish, there's no lobster, so he can't be cruel to it. Secondly, the worst thing that can happen is he falls overboard.'

'I never thought o' that.' Hamish narrowed his eyes at the reporter.

'Look, I've taken it a few times and there's nothing wrong with me.'

'That's a matter o' debate. Tae poison the skipper o' a vessel when it's lost in a blizzard isna normal behaviour as far as I'm concerned. You should be ashamed of yourself!' With that he disappeared back through the hatch.

When Hamish first scanned the snowy deck, his heart sank, for he could see no sign of Hoynes. It was only when he glimpsed the end of a long boat hook appearing above the wheelhouse did he realise that, far from falling overboard, Hoynes was still pursuing the lobster.

Hamish hurried round the back of the wheelhouse and, sure enough, there he was, brandishing the boat hook wildly, as snow gathered on top of his bunnet.

'Right,' said Hamish, sensing that it was time to take direct action. 'I've a plan.'

Hoynes looked him up and down. 'Why are you dressed in your faither's suit?'

'What? Oh, aye,' said Hamish, playing along. 'Nice day to gie it an airing.'

'I know what you're at. Trying tae impress that wee lassie instead o' helping me subdue this monster. It's already had a couple o' goes at me wae they claws, but I managed tae evade them. Jeest in the nick o' time, though.' He gave Hamish a wild-eyed look.

'I've had an idea, Sandy. Why don't you head down below? This beast's intentions are clearly malign, so he'll likely chase you – and when he does I'll whack it o'er the heid wae something substantial.'

Hoynes looked at him as though working out a complex calculation in his head. His forefinger darted to and fro as the choreography of Hamish's plan played out across his mind's eye.

'What dae you think?'

'I reckon your plan might jeest work, Hamish,' Hoynes whispered.

'Why are you whispering?'

'Are you daft? He can hear us! That bloody thing's as fluent as you. It must have been brought up in the sea at Firdale, for he has a fair twang.'

'You've spoken tae him?'

'Och, we passed the time o' day and the like. He's never seen weather like this, neither. Quite cordial, he was, but I sense it's jeest an act.' He lowered his voice further. 'On the count o' three I'll make a break for the hatch.'

'Right you are, skipper,' said Hamish, with an enthusiasm he didn't feel.

Without counting to three, Hoynes suddenly threw the boat hook to the deck and scurried off towards the cabin hatch. But instead of lowering himself feet first, Hoynes clasped his hands together as though in prayer and dived, head first, through the opening. For a moment, his girth held him fast in its narrow confines. But gravity soon did its work and, before Hamish could grab his legs, his skipper tumbled into the cabin.

'What happened?' shouted Jo.

'I dread tae think,' said Hamish, lowering himself down beside his skipper.

# 15

The old quay in Kinloch harbour was thronged with people. Constable Mann was there, so was the senior fire officer, Andy Semple. Doctor Fraser's face bore a grave expression, as he puffed on his Woodbine. Peter Mitchell, the harbour master, who was staring desperately out over the loch, shook his head, as the snow piled up on the pier.

Provost McMurdo, too, looked concerned, for such snow-fall had rarely been seen on the peninsula. He turned to Mitchell. 'And conditions are worse out in the sound, apparently?'

'Aye, ten times worse. I've just had Davie Robertson on the radio. The signal is terrible because of the snow. But he and the rest of the fleet have turned round.'

'All apart from Hoynes, that is?'

'Aye. That thrawn old bugger refuses to carry a radio aboard. He says it upsets the fish.'

'Well, he's more than fish to worry him now.' The provost lowered his head.

Senga Murray, the matron of the cottage hospital, sighed. 'Would you look at you all! Job's comforters, and no mistake. Sandy Hoynes might not have a radio, but he's the best sailor for miles around. There's no' an inch o' that coast he's no' acquainted with, and you know it. If any man can bring us supplies, it'll be him.'

The provost, the doctor, the police constable, harbour master and fire officer looked at each other, their faces all bearing doubtful expressions.

'My goodness, men are big on drama, and that's a fact,' declared Matron Murray. 'It's the same in the hospital. You get a man in wae a skelf in his finger and you'd think a tree had fallen on his head, while a woman will drag the thing oot wae a pair o' tweezers while engaging in some healthy gossip on the phone.'

'God willing, the rest of the boys will make it back. As soon as the weather clears, we'll get them and the lifeboat out and look for poor Hoynes. It's all we can do,' said the harbour master.

'We should sing a hymn,' said the town clerk, who was a pious man.

'For any sake,' muttered the matron. 'Should we no' jeest go the whole hog and start flinging flowers into the loch?'

'No' a bad idea,' said Semple, whose wife owned the florist.

'Wait!' shouted Mitchell. 'I see a boat coming past the island. I think it's the *Dark Isle*.'

The little crowd squinted into the snow, as the shape of one fishing boat then another emerged from the blizzard. One by one, Kinloch's fishing fleet straggled back into the loch to a hearty cheer from all those looking on. All except for the *Girl Maggie*, that is.

❄

At the head of the quay, sheltered beneath the eaves of the Mission, gathered the old fishermen. Though not in direct contact with the great and the good of the community further down the pier, they knew the score.

Peeny stroked his chin, as the fishing boats tied up. 'Och, I knew fine this was an ill-conceived idea, right fae the start.'

'And right you were,' said Malcolm Connelly. 'You canna trust a forecast these days. Och, it's one o' they once-in-a-lifetime events. We've all seen them before.'

'If we've seen them before they can hardly be once in a lifetime,' quipped Peeny, who hid a tendency for pedantry under a façade of bonhomie.

'Hoynes will be ploughing on regardless,' said McKirdy. 'I canna blame him for no' wanting to have a radio aboard. We all know fine it's jeest another ploy so the fishery officer can keep tabs on you. They buggers would stalk their ain granny if they thought she was wandering oot the chip shop wae an understated quantity o' fish in her supper.'

Peeny sighed. 'Sandy won't be fazed by the snow. He's the last o' the true fishermen, and that's a fact. He could get you fae here to New York and no' consult a chart at all.'

'He'd need a fair stock o' whisky for that passage, mind you,' said Connelly.

'I can jeest picture the scene aboard the *Girl Maggie* now,' said McKirdy. 'Big Sandy staring intae the blizzard using all his senses tae overcome the worst that nature can throw at him. He'll put the likes o' McMichael – who's no' half the fisherman his faither was – and wee Robertson tae shame.'

There was a general murmur of consensus, before the collective decision was made to decamp to the County and ponder on Hoynes' route to Girvan.

❄

Aboard the *Girl Maggie*, though, things could not have been less like the imaginings of the old seadogs back in Kinloch. It was Hamish who stood in the wheelhouse squinting into the snow. Despite the bitter cold, a bead of sweat made its way down his forehead from under his cap.

That he knew the sea and the ways of navigation, there was no doubt. But he'd no experience sailing in heavy snow. He knew he should trust in the compass, but it was only as good as Hoynes' last reading, and that had been right at the very beginning of their journey and was hardly ideal. He couldn't see the sun behind the blanket of snow. Everything was just . . . white.

In ordinary conditions, he'd have been busy keeping the lines and deck clear of snow. But with Hoynes incapacitated in the cabin, the white stuff was piling up so quickly it was hard to determine the shape of the boat at all. The *Girl Maggie* was beginning to look like a floating snowball.

Hamish was also fretting over something else. Hoynes' vessel was sturdy, well designed for its fishing duties, but it most certainly was not built for speed. Most of Kinloch's fleet was made up of newer, faster boats. They were slow to start, but once they made their way into open water Hamish calculated that they should have caught up with the *Girl Maggie* long ago. He'd called them repeatedly through the loud hailer, but to no avail, and the silence only multiplied his woes.

Hamish brushed the sweat from his forehead and reached for the speaking tube. He'd instructed Jo to keep an eye on Hoynes. To the best of his ability, he'd made sure his stricken skipper had no broken bones, and managed – with no little effort, it had to be said – to manhandle the older man's bulky frame into the bottom bunk where Jo had been trying to shake off her seasickness. She was now slumped near the other end of the speaking tube, keeping an eye on Hoynes.

'Has he moved yet?' Hamish shouted into the mouthpiece.

It took a few moments for her to master the basic technology, but soon her voice sounded weakly in the wheelhouse. 'No change, he's just lying there. His eye twitched a couple of times, but that's all.'

'Well, at least he's no' deid,' said Hamish. 'Is this what normally happens wae folk that's taken this DSL?'

'It's LSD! And people react in different ways. I'm no expert, I've only taken it a couple of times myself.'

'And what happened tae you?'

'It was . . .'

'What?'

'Kind of – sexual.'

'I never heard such talk! I'm sure the skipper isn't experiencing anything o' the kind. Wherever this poison has taken him, it'll be wholesome, I can assure you o' that!'

'And how do you know he's out cold because of LSD? It could just as easily be down to the fall. He took a right thump.'

'My, but you're a cheery soul, right enough. As if I hadna enough tae worry me up here.'

'Surely we've passed Arran by now?'

'I would hope so. Now all we have to worry aboot is crashing intae Ayrshire. Do you think you're fit tae come up on deck for a while?'

'To do what?'

'Man the wheel while I check on Sandy.'

'I'd be womaning the wheel. And even if I could make it, I've never steered a boat in my life.'

'There's nothing to it at all – well, unless we hit something. I'll only be away for a couple o' minutes.'

'I'll try. But I can't promise not to be sick all over your wheelhouse.'

Hamish replaced the speaking tube on its hook and squinted into the blizzard. Their only chance of salvation now was the Girvan lighthouse.

# 16

An impromptu emergency meeting was taking place in the bar at the County Hotel. It consisted of the harbour master, the provost, the town clerk and fishermen young and old. The fire was blazing, and each man had a large dram before him, but the mood was one of gloomy resignation.

The phone at the bar rang.

'It's for you, Peter,' said the barman.

Mitchell got to his feet and had to lean across the bar, as the flex on the phone was rather too short for purpose. He frowned as he listened intently to what was being said. By turns, he nodded, shook his head, pursed his lips, rubbed his temples and grimaced. 'Thank you, Wattie. Just keep looking. We'd be most obliged.'

He turned to the gathering. 'It was the Coastguard at Girvan. They've sent some boats out as far as they dare, sounding their horns, making enough noise to raise the dead. But not a peep from Hoynes.'

'He'd no' be the length o' Girvan yet. No' in this weather. He'll have tae take it slow.'

'But even saying he is, he should be in the vicinity of the search vessels and the lifeboat soon.'

Peeny looked at the clock above the bar. 'I would gie them

another hour. Hoynes is a cautious man, for all his bluster. He'll be taking it sure and steady. Dae we have any word on the weather, Peter?'

'According tae the Met Office, it's in for the day, aye, and most o' the night.'

'If it gets dark, Hoynes will surely weigh anchor if he hasn't hit land?' said McMichael.

'"Hit" being the operative word. He could easily jeest sail intae they rocks at Culzean, or anywhere. If I were him I'd be at anchor right noo, trying tae sit this out.'

'Wait!' exclaimed Davie Robertson. 'They might no' have a radio aboard, but they have a wireless.'

'And what difference will that make?' asked Mitchell.

'We could get a message tae them – over the air, so tae speak.'

All eyes turned to Provost McMurdo. He looked back at them through sad, rheumy eyes. 'What do you want me to do?'

'Get a haud o' they radio folk. Get them tae tell Hoynes tae stay at anchor until this clears – if the idea hasn't crossed his mind yet.'

'That's all very well. But what station does he listen to?'

'Och, it'll be the Home Service. Every fisherman listens tae that for the shipping forecasts,' said Peeny.

'It's got a new-fangled name now,' said McMichael. 'A number. Mind they changed it all earlier this year.'

'Right enough. So all they weans can listen tae that racket. No' a decent accordion or fiddle to be heard,' said McKirdy.

'That'll be Radio One,' observed Peeny, to the surprise of everyone. 'I'm quite partial tae thon Seekers. Right good harmonies, so they have.'

A moment's hush fell over the room, as those gathered took stock of this unexpected piece of information.

'So you want me to phone the BBC and get them to broadcast a distress call?' said McMurdo.

'That should suffice. I mean, surely Hoynes has had the wireless on, monitoring the forecast anyway,' said Mitchell. 'A wee prompt would do no harm.'

'Right. I'll get back to my office and see what I can do.' The provost hurried from the bar, closely followed by the town clerk.

'Ach, we've likely saved the day,' said McKirdy. 'They call it a brains trust.'

Harbour Master Peter Mitchell looked about those assembled. 'Aye, something like that,' he said, with little conviction.

❄

Hamish was now in the cabin, his hand on Sandy Hoynes' forehead, checking to see if he was feverish. It felt fine to the fisherman, but he wasn't sure he had sufficient experience in medical care to make an informed diagnosis. Certainly, the skipper looked peaceful enough; as Jo had mentioned, his left eye was twitching from time to time, so at least he was still alive.

Hamish knew he couldn't leave Jo at the wheel for long. Desperately, he racked his brain to think of something to do that might ease their plight. He nudged Hoynes a couple of times, but no response was forthcoming.

Then something dawned on him: Hoynes loved music. If anything was likely to bring him round, surely a good tune would be the very thing. He jumped from his skipper's side and was up and through the hatch with a fluidity of movement that would have done a pole vaulter credit.

Crumping through the snow, he was dismayed to see Jo slumped over the wheel. 'My goodness, lassie! Have you been like this the whole time I've been below?'

She shook her head. 'No, but it's worse up here. We're rolling about in nothingness. It's like some nightmare.'

'Have you set eyes on anything? The Girvan light, for example?'

'No, just snow.'

Hamish reached behind her and grabbed the dilapidated transistor radio from a shelf in the wheelhouse. 'I'm going to play some music tae Sandy. He's fair fond o' a tune. It might be the very thing tae bring him round. I've seen it done wae folk in a coma at the pictures. You'll have tae hang on for a couple mair minutes.'

She nodded feebly as Hamish once more disappeared through the hatch.

# 17

Back at the town hall, Provost McMurdo was looking at a large map of Kintyre, and the route they all hoped Hoynes was taking to the Ayrshire coast. To his untrained eye it all looked really simple – almost a straight line, in fact. But as the seamen had reminded him, there were many hidden obstacles and dangers lurking in the wide expanse of blue that appeared so benign on the map. And that was without factoring in the driving snow.

He looked outside just as old Mr Henderson took an impromptu dive outside Morrison's the barber. Thankfully, the gentleman's fall was broken by the great accumulation on Main Street. As Henderson brushed himself down, he must have sensed McMurdo's eyes on him. He glared up at the provost, and McMurdo waved at him by way of consolation. In return, Henderson raised two fingers and shuffled off down the street, though in a more tentative manner.

McMurdo shook his head. He wasn't native to Kinloch, having arrived forty years before as a keen young veterinarian. Now retired, he sometimes wondered why he'd taken to local politics. There was little doubt that it was an often thankless task. The burdens and irritations of the office were many. But now he felt as though he had the people's lives on his conscience, and that was not a happy place in which to dwell.

The phone on his desk rang twice, indicating an internal call. 'Yes, please go ahead.'

'I have a producer from the BBC on the line for you,' announced the town clerk.

'Good. What's his name?'

'I'm rather surprised to say that it's a young lady, a Miss Thomson.'

'Why are you surprised?'

'Och, I don't know. You just imagine a man in a responsible job like that.'

'I have to say, it's high time you altered your attitude. One of these days we'll have a female provost – maybe even a prime minister.' He heard the town clerk snort with derision. 'Put her through. And try to drag yourself into this decade, man!'

There followed a click or two, then Miss Thomson introduced herself in clipped tones that made McMurdo instinctively sit up straight in his high-backed chair.

'I understand you have an emergency you would like us to help with, Mr McMurdo?'

'Yes, we do have a bit of a situation on the go. One of our fishing vessels is somewhere between here and Girvan in a blizzard. They have no radio, but they do have a wireless. We were thinking that perhaps you could pass on a message over the airwaves, so to speak.'

'I believe the weather with you is somewhat inclement. Strange time to go fishing.'

'Yes, it's dire, in fact. That's the real problem. They're not out fishing, but on a mercy mission of sorts.'

'A mercy mission? Do tell.'

'I'm not sure how well acquainted you are with the

**97**

geography here. But we're rather out on a limb. With the level of snowfall, the peninsula could be cut off for weeks. Mr Hoynes and his crew, along with the rest of the fishing fleet, volunteered to sail to the Ayrshire coast to bring back much-needed supplies. Hoynes aside, they all turned back because of the weather, but the *Girl Maggie* is still out there.'

There was silence on the other end of the phone for a few moments, then Thomson spoke. 'So what you're telling me is that these men are heroes.'

'Well, yes, I suppose I am.'

'Now that's a real story! Leave this with me, Mr McMurdo. I'll be back with you within the hour.'

'Oh, right,' said McMurdo, slightly taken aback. 'I'll await your call.'

He put the phone down and glanced out the window. Snow was still falling thick and fast. He took a cigar from the box hidden in a drawer, lit it and puffed it into life. Outside in the community, McMurdo always smoked a pipe. But in the privacy of his office or at home, he secretly enjoyed a cigar much more. Unfortunately, those in Kinloch whom he served would have considered such a habit unforgivably bourgeois, so, in public, it was pipe only.

As he watched the cloud of smoke curl round the room, he considered the conversation he'd just had with the BBC radio producer. Then he pictured Sandy Hoynes and his reputation for skulduggery, not to mention his fondness for strong drink. Though he was desperate to see the *Girl Maggie* safely back in port, the thought of her skipper becoming the face of the town in the national media was not a welcome one.

He reached into another drawer and produced a bottle of whisky and a glass. He poured himself a large measure and silently wished he'd listened to his wife and retired to a holiday home in France rather than become Kinloch's political master. For in reality, nobody could master this place.

✳

Hoynes lay in his bunk in the cabin of the *Girl Maggie*, the sublime strains of Mozart sounding incongruously grand in such a small, dishevelled space.

At the chart table, Jo had perked up a little. Her trip up on deck had made her feel distinctly worse, but back in the cabin, nursing a mug of Hamish's strong tea, she felt herself a little restored. As she looked at Hoynes' recumbent figure, she observed no change. He lay stock still, apart from a flickering left eyelid.

Now, though she'd been aware of it all the time but too squeamish to care, their perilous situation dawned on her. Here they were on a tiny fishing boat, with no real clue as to their position. Not only that, the captain of the vessel was indisposed by ingestion of a hallucinogenic and an unfortunate plummet through the hatch. Though Hamish made reassuring noises, she could tell by his worried expression that he was less than confident of his ability to bring them safely to port, never mind find it.

The radio, though, was soothing. Jo closed her eyes and let the music wash over her. It had been an early start, and her eyes were heavy from lack of sleep and the draining effect of seasickness. Her head was drooping forwards when what she heard over the radio brought her back to full wakefulness.

'*And this is a message to the fishing boat* Girl Maggie *and her crew. From all of us here at the BBC, and I daresay the whole nation, we wish you well. The advice from the harbour master at Kinloch is to weigh anchor and ride out the storm. And from us to you, on this brave mercy mission to feed the good people of Kintyre, here is the organist and choir from King's College, Cambridge, with that wonderful hymn to mariners everywhere, "For Those In Peril On the Sea". May God bless you and bring you back safely to port.'*

At first Jo couldn't believe her ears. Perhaps it was exhaustion – or the realisation of their desperate plight – that had led her to imagine such a message echoing from the wireless. But the hymn was still playing through the crackle of static.

She reached for the speaking tube and hailed Hamish.

'Is he awake?' asked the first mate hopefully.

'No, but I've just heard a message from the harbour master at Kinloch on the radio. You've to weigh anchor and ride out the storm.'

'Have you been at the drugs, tae? Am I the only sane person aboard this vessel?'

'No, honestly, I heard it!'

Hamish was about to reply when he heard a commotion from the cabin below. It came in the form of a scream that would curdle the blood. 'What on earth is happening down there?'

'It's Mr Hoynes. He's sitting up in the bunk and staring at his hands.'

# 18

When Hoynes first became aware of the music, he shot up in his bunk. Everything seemed familiar. He was fully aware that he was aboard the *Girl Maggie*, though his memory was hazy as to why he was in the cabin. He had a thumping pain in his head, and felt the need to rub his temples with thumb and forefinger, a trick of headache relief his grandmother had shown him, and by which he swore.

But when he removed his right hand from under the dun woollen blanket his eyes widened in horror. For this was no hand – no human hand, at least. It was a gigantic lobster claw at the end of his arm. For a split second he was paralysed by fear, then he screamed, hearing his own voice echo round the tiny cabin. As he did so, he saw the lobster claw flex in a snapping motion.

He stopped screaming and made to move his other arm. But a figure appearing before him made him freeze.

'Sandy, thank the Lord you're okay!' Hamish stared down at his skipper with a benign expression.

Hoynes gazed at the apparition in front of him. Though strangely familiar, the vision of the deformed face was hideous. The sallow face with the slanting eyes was plain enough, but instead of hair, two curling horns like that of a seasoned ram emerged from the top of his head. To top off this terrifying spectacle, the man with the horns, who stood only feet away from him now, was dressed in the full garb of a man of the cloth. He wore a dark grey suit, under which was a black shirt with a white dog collar.

'Jeest you stay where you are!' screamed Hoynes, thrusting his large claw out before him for protection against this foul apparition.

'It's me, Hamish – your first mate, skipper.'

Hoynes saw the creature's lips move, but all he heard was a jumble of sounds that made no sense. He backed as far away as the cramped space of his bunk would allow, making sure he held out his claw before him, snapping it at the horned minister to discourage him from coming any nearer. He heard himself scream again, so loudly that the sound made his eyes vibrate and the vision before him shimmer in the gloom.

❄

Hamish looked at Jo. 'What on earth is wrong wae the skipper?' He stared back at the man he knew so well. Hoynes' face bore an expression of abject terror, his fingers snapping together like a puppeteer with his hand in a sock.

The commotion had done enough to banish Jo's nausea and the journalist in her began to kick in. 'He's having a bad trip, Hamish.'

'It's no' been a joyride for me either.'

'No. I mean the drug. He's probably hallucinating.'

'The poor bugger has taken leave o' his senses, that's mair like it. What have you done to him?'

Hoynes screamed again, this time grabbing the old blanket

and pulling it over his face to banish the vision of horror before him. But his hand still snapped at the edge of the blanket, and his sea boots now protruded from beneath it at the bottom end of the bunk.

'It'll wear off. Try not to worry.'

'Try not to worry! My skipper's turned intae a raving imbecile and we're lost at sea in a blizzard. I would say I've every right tae be worried, wouldn't you?'

Jo ignored Hamish and edged towards her bag, where her notepad, pens and camera were kept.

'What are you at?'

'I'm going to get a picture of this. I'm sure the paper can use it in some way or other.'

But before she could get to the bag, Hamish lurched forwards and grabbed it from her by the strap.

'You're responsible for this predicament. You'll no' be taking any pictures o' my skipper while he's no' in his right mind.'

Jo shot from her sea chair and began tussling with Hamish over the tools of her trade.

❄

Hoynes could hear a commotion of sorts, though what was being said was still just an incomprehensible jumble. He made sure that, even though his head was beneath the blanket, his claw was flicking to and fro above his head to deter the fiendish minister.

But despite his fear and disorientation, he couldn't resist having a look over the edge of the blanket. He could see two figures wrestling with each other. The man appeared to be holding a baby, while an elderly woman was trying to drag it from his grasp.

The more he stared, the more he recognised the slight figure. It was his mother! It was then the thought crossed his mind. His poor mother was fighting to save her child from the beast with the horns. And something in him understood that the babe in arms was none other than himself. He had to help her!

Hoynes was about to force himself from the bed when his gaze landed on something else. At the bottom of the bunk where his feet should have been was a massive lobster tail. When he tried to move, the tail jolted up and down as though he was trying to scuttle away on a sandy seabed.

He opened his mouth and screamed again.

❄

Hamish was hauling at the strap, but Jo had a firm grip of her bag. She was surprisingly strong for a slip of a lassie, he thought. But just as he was gaining ground, Hoynes, hitherto silent in the bunk apart from his flicking hand, let out a yell that, if anything, was louder and even more blood-curdling than the last.

The sudden scream made Jo let go of the bag, and the surprise of this caught Hamish unawares. Suddenly pulling against fresh air, he toppled backwards and hit his head off the stove.

Jo looked from one fisherman to the other. Hoynes was back under his blanket, fingers snapping frantically in the air, while Hamish was out cold, motionless beside the stove.

'Shit!' she said loudly, making Hoynes retreat further into the safety of his bunk.

She knelt over Hamish, first of all checking his pulse to

make sure the blow hadn't been fatal. Thankfully, his heartbeat was strong, though he was unconscious. It was then that the full horror of her predicament dawned. She was aboard a boat, sailing through a blizzard, with both captain and first mate incapacitated.

Jo tried speaking into Hamish's left ear, but no response was forthcoming. Gently, she slid her hand under his head, mercifully not encountering the wet stickiness of warm blood she'd expected.

As a keen Girl Guide, she knew some basic survival techniques. Carefully, recalling her first aid badge, she rolled Hamish over on his side, making sure that if he was sick he wouldn't choke. Examining the back of his head once more, she was further relieved that there appeared to be no sign of blood. Though an egg-shaped lump was plain under his thinning hair.

She spoke to the fisherman once more, gave him a gentle shake, but there was no response.

Jo felt her stomach lurch, as though she was on a roller-coaster or in a rapidly descending lift. She thought at first it was just a nervous reaction to her situation, but when a tin mug was dislodged from its hook, she realised that the boat itself had began to move most alarmingly.

Making one last attempt to rouse Hamish, and failing, she looked across at the mound under the woollen blanket that was Sandy Hoynes. His hand still grabbed at the air, and she could see his legs were trembling.

Realising there was no other option, she made for the hatch and, with the help of a chair, managed to haul herself through it.

# 19

Back in Kinloch, the snow was still falling.

In the town hall, Provost McMurdo had long since stopped taking calls. Since the plight of the *Girl Maggie* had been aired on national radio, it appeared as though Hoynes had become a hero the length and breadth of the country. He'd had calls from newspapers, television companies, even *Fisherman's Weekly*, all wanting to know more of the plight of what was now Kinloch's most famous vessel.

He heard the phone ring again in the town clerk's office and sighed. He'd spent much of the afternoon speaking to the Coastguard, the RNLI and even the Minister of Agriculture and Fisheries. The general consensus was that nothing could be done now that darkness had descended upon the town. They had reached the conclusion that come the morning – in the hope that the snow would have stopped, or at least lessened – a search for the *Girl Maggie* would begin. Two Royal Navy helicopters had been promised, should visibility be suitable, and the town's fishing fleet, alongside the lifeboat and their opposite numbers in Girvan, would all put to sea in an attempt to trace the missing vessel. There was even a destroyer steaming towards the area, though like the rest of the rescue party they wouldn't be able to search in earnest until first light.

It appeared that even radar wasn't working properly in these extreme weather conditions.

Burdened by guilt, McMurdo tried to console himself that he'd tried his best to mitigate the situation. But still the feeling that he was responsible for Hoynes' plight gnawed away at him.

Though he was no career politician, he realised the last thing he should do was hide away in the town hall. So McMurdo made the decision to head to the heart of the fishing community – doubtless next door in the County Hotel, he reckoned. He pulled his heavy overcoat from its hook and placed his trilby firmly on his head. Checking himself in the mirror, he made sure that his tie was straight under his starched collar, and again noticed the resemblance many had commented on over the years between himself and Neville Chamberlain. It was part of the reason he'd entered local politics in the first place.

Right now, he wished he looked more like Frankie Howerd.

He leaned his head into the town clerk's office. 'I'm going out for a short while.'

'Are you going to be some time?' replied his junior, casting a look at the big flakes falling under the glow of the streetlights.

'Very funny. If I'm Captain Oates, just work out who you are in the story.'

Without further comment, McMurdo took to the stairs. He'd never liked his assistant, who was a civil servant rather than an elected politician. Though he had the power of the local council, the town clerk had a healthy salary, and a decent pension to look forward to. McMurdo felt that this, and the fact that his post was permanent, made him feel superior to the provost. In any event, he made sure that the town clerk was kept on his toes, and there was little doubt he had to work hard for his money.

Outside on Main Street, even the path dug through the snow by the Machrie miners would have been barely visible had it not been for the massive heaps of the white stuff on each of its sides. He felt strange walking past the ground-floor windows of the town hall. It was as though he had become taller and was looking at a smaller building altogether. The fact was, a good few feet of it were now under the tightly packed snow.

The County Hotel was only a few yards away, but McMurdo took this short journey steadily, anxious not to fall and hurt himself. The town needed its leader at this time, of that he was in no doubt.

He hadn't known quite what to expect when he entered the bar, but still he was surprised by how empty it was. Normally in times of crisis locals flocked to the town's pubs for news and to have a good gossip as to the likely outcome of this or that. Of course, the opinions agreed upon were usually of the gloomy variety, but such was the temper of a small community.

Only two men sat at the bar, Peeny and McKirdy. Though they differed in appearance – McKirdy being tall and broad, Peeny slight, with a pinched face – they were easily marked out as part of the fishing community by virtue of their weathered faces and deliberate manner. Most fishermen seemed to weigh their words before they spoke, seemingly swirling them round their mind like a connoisseur might savour a fine brandy before swallowing. He supposed this came of so much time spent at sea alone with their thoughts.

'Gentlemen,' said McMurdo, brushing the snow from his coat

to the floor and engendering a glower from the barman. 'I hope I can buy you a drink?'

'Your hope is not in vain, Mr McMurdo. We'll take as much drink as you can afford, for this is a black day for Kinloch's fishing fleet,' said Peeny with a sigh and a shake of the head.

'Mair like a white day, I'd say,' said McKirdy. 'I've never seen snow like it. No' here, at any rate.'

'Aye, it's the kind o' scenario you might encounter up the Matterhorn, or the likes. But no' here at Kinloch. It's jeest no' natural at all.'

'But you surely believe that Mr Hoynes will have taken the appropriate steps. After all, he's a very experienced mariner.'

Peeny stroked his stubbly chin. 'Aye, but he's an impetuous man. You jeest had tae see that race he had wae McMichael this morning tae know that. A man o' his age should be taking his time, no' rushing off like Francis Chichester.'

'Maybe if he'd been one o' the slower boats oot o' the loch, he might no' be in the predicament in which he finds himself now – fair afloat on a dark ocean, wae the burden o' snow all around. A man can make mistakes in weather like that – aye, even an experienced one.'

'Plus he and Hamish will be drunk as lords by now,' added Peeny.

'Surely you don't think they'll have partaken in strong drink, not in the danger they're in?' McMurdo was beginning to wish he'd stayed in his office. These gloomy predictions were doing nothing for his feelings of guilt.

'It'll be like this, Mr McMurdo. Hoynes will easily see the hopelessness o' his situation and have cracked open a bottle as soon as it got dark. He'll be anchored – if he can, that is.

And that's when hope begins tae drift.' McKirdy nodded his head mournfully.

McMurdo knocked back the whisky he'd just been given and held out his glass for a refill. One thing was certain, he needed something to bolster his morale.

'Of course, they may well have made land,' said McKirdy.

'Oh well, that would be good.' Suddenly McMurdo felt a surge of confidence.

'No' if land is a great sheet o' rocks or a length o' shingle under some great cliff.'

'What would happen then?'

'If they survived the impact, they're likely out cold on a beach burning the boat for warmth tae try and attract some attention.'

'Hang on, McKirdy,' said Peeny. 'That's a right doleful thought.'

McMurdo breathed a sigh of relief at this.

'They could jeest as easy be clinging on tae some rock face for dear life. Or perhaps they've constructed one o' they igloos. I'm sure Sandy will be acquainted wae the mechanics involved. After all, he knows about every other bloody thing!'

'Come, gentlemen, I'm sure things can't be as black as you paint them.'

'Och, that's no' half as black as they could get. Man, they could collide wae some great cargo vessel and cause an international incident, or one o' they oil tankers. The loch would be pure oil, if that happened.' Peeny nodded sagely.

McMurdo threw another large measure down his throat. He had an analytical mind, and it didn't take much mental effort to realise that if such a calamity did occur, the blame would be placed firmly at his door. How he wished he'd never encouraged the fleet to take to sea. The town could easily have survived a while longer. His actions had been impetuous.

He felt he had to try to change the subject, so looking around the room he commented on the absence of customers.

McKirdy looked at him as though he was mad. 'You canna expect folk tae come rushing oot in weather like this, Mr McMurdo!'

'Well, you're both here.'

'Aye, that's fair. But I live across the street and Peeny's flat's at the back o' the car park. The place is on oor doorsteps.' Both he and Peeny shook their heads at the provost's lack of common sense.

Being assured now that the County had little to offer in terms of succour or respite, McMurdo walked to the stand and hefted his coat back on. The snow that had gathered on it had melted in the warmth of the bar, and it was now unpleasantly damp. 'I'll bid you a good evening, gents,' he said, with a tip of his trilby. 'Another two large measures for my friends, please.' He passed the requisite money across the bar and made for the door, and onwards to his office in the gloomy town hall.

'Aye, but you're a fine man, Mr McMurdo,' said Peeny.

'Jeest the best!' opined McKirdy.

They craned their necks through the serving hatch into the hotel lobby to make sure the town's provost was leaving the premises.

'Aye, a right useless bugger, he is,' said McKirdy.

'A waste o' space, to be sure. It's no' a man like that you need in times o' a crisis. They tell me young Charlie Murray the joiner has his eyes on the job.'

'He's hardly mair than a boy.'

'Think o' Pitt the Younger, McKirdy. He was a wean when he became prime minister o' the country, so they say.'

McKirdy considered this. 'Aye, but that's an easy job compared wae being the provost o' Kinloch. We both know it.'

The pair nodded in silent agreement and, as though choreographed, knocked back the whiskies bought by the man they'd just derided, in absolute unison.

# 20

Jo had done her best to make Hamish comfortable by placing a pillow under his head. She was glad to hear him groan and mutter as she did this, and hoped beyond hope that he would regain his senses before long. As for Hoynes, he was clearly conscious, but still not in his right mind.

She remembered that they'd said on the wireless that the vessel should weigh anchor. She guessed this meant chucking a large cast-iron implement overboard, but reasoned that there was no way she could lift it. And, in any case, it was nowhere to be seen under the deep snow on deck.

When first she ventured up, following Hamish's accident, she noticed the heavy swell was making the wheel swing to and fro, as if by its own accord. Jo had been taking driving lessons recently and, even though she was in a boat, rather than a Hillman Imp, she realised that this likely meant that the craft was describing a meandering path over the waves.

It was time to make a decision.

She knew enough to work out that an unanchored vessel would drift in any direction that took the tide's fancy. This meant they could be dashed against rocks, sandbanks or the other hazards she'd heard mentioned during her short time at sea.

Jo thought hard about what the driving instructor back in Glasgow had taught her. If you wanted to turn in a circle, the wheel should be turned to its full extent, one way or the other. She grabbed the wheel in the small cabin and swung the wheel to her left. Yes, she could feel the direction of the vessel change!

Finally, after many more turns than it would take the steering wheel of a car to reach its full extent, it stopped. Jo could now picture the *Girl Maggie* travelling in circles on the dark sea. This wasn't ideal, she knew, but at least it reduced the chance of drifting or ploughing into something while travelling forwards.

She tethered the wheel to a hook on the wheelhouse window with a length of old rope she found in the cabin, and then pulled back on the handle she'd seen both Hoynes and Hamish use to alter the speed. Sure enough, Jo heard the tone of the engine drop and the vessel slowed down.

Confident she'd done the best she could, Jo checked that the lights were still showing fore and aft, and, shivering in the cold, returned to the cabin and the indisposed crew. She was still worried that another vessel could collide with the *Girl Maggie*, but surely no sailors would be abroad on such a night.

Jo huddled by the stove, after piling in more coal. She was hungry, thirsty, miserable and scared. But then she heard something.

In the gloom she saw a shape emerge from the bottom bunk.

'Mr Hoynes, are you okay?'

Silence.

'Mr Hoynes, it's okay to come and sit over here.' She hoped gentle encouragement would help the skipper to calm down.

Hoynes' figure remained stock still for a few moments, then slowly he eased himself off the bunk.

'Is that you, Mother?'

Jo sighed. She'd hoped he'd have regained his senses. 'No, it's me, Jo Baird from the *Glasgow Times*, do you remember?'

A pause. 'Aye, of course I remember. The wee lassie. A right scunner you are, too. Man, but I've been having such dreams. How long have I been asleep?'

'It's a long story, Mr Hoynes.'

The skipper appeared in the dim light of the oil lamp hanging above the stove. 'What on earth is Hamish doing doon there?'

'He fell and hit his head. I'm quite worried about him.'

Hoynes knelt over his shipmate. 'Well, he's still breathing, at least.' He nudged Hamish with the toe of his boot. The younger man stirred, mumbled something incoherent, and was again still. 'How long has he been like this?'

'I don't know, an hour – hour and a half, maybe?'

Hoynes raised his head, a puzzled look on his face. 'And tell me something else. Why are we going round in circles?'

'You can tell?' Jo was impressed. 'Ah, now you'll have to let me explain.'

Hoynes listened with mounting alarm as Jo described the last few hours. Though she skirted over the real reasons for his temporary incapacitation, blaming it on the fall, the real danger they were in quickly dawned on the skipper.

'You stay here with Hamish and I'll get up there and weigh the anchor.'

'How will you manage? I couldn't even see it under all that snow.'

'Don't worry aboot that. I've been a long time at this, you know.' With that he squeezed through the hatch.

As Jo looked on, she doubted she'd been as relieved by

anything in her life. She stared at Hamish, who looked pale in the gloom. Now all she had to do was reinvigorate him and her job here would be done. She switched on the wireless just as the shipping forecast began its ritualised meander around the nation's coast.

Then she remembered the job she'd been sent here to do. Clearly, there were things she couldn't put in print, but she was in no doubt – redacted as it would have to be – that this would make a fantastic story. Especially now they had been on the wireless. She reached into her bag for her notepad.

❄

Hoynes stared through the dark and the snow at the deck of the fishing boat he knew so well, illuminated only by a single storm lantern. Had a photograph of this been presented to him, he would have been hard pressed to identify it as a seagoing vessel, never mind his own.

His thoughts were still rather jumbled, and for some reason he couldn't stop thinking about lobsters, but their current predicament was foremost in his mind. Jo had told him about the messages broadcast on the wireless, and while he felt a certain pride in this he was amazed they'd made it as far as they had without calamity.

It was cold, but Hoynes was sure the anchor would still work. Its weight would be sufficient to dislodge the snow, and it was unlikely to be frozen. He stopped the engine, then hauled on the handle to release the anchor. At first his heart missed a beat, but after a few moments the familiar sound of the chain releasing the robust anchor from the bow could be heard, snow muffling the usual clanking.

He had no idea where they were. Yes, he could see the compass, but that only spoke of which way they were now pointing. He'd no notion of how far they'd sailed, or in which direction. In normal circumstances, even below, he'd have been able to tell by virtue of instinct and experience whether or not the boat had drifted off course. But as he'd been unconscious, or at least not in his right mind, he'd been deprived of this sixth sense. He was still unsure quite why he'd suffered such an affliction, and vowed to press Jo on it when they were safely in port, as her explanation had been sketchy to say the least.

Hoynes leaned on the ledge beside the ship's wheel, still jury-rigged by the rope his passenger had used to make them sail in circles. Aye, he thought. She may have no experience of the sea, but there was nothing wrong with her reasoning.

His choices were limited. They could try to plough on when the day dawned, but if the snow continued like this, there was little point. He'd have to sit at anchor until either the weather improved, or rescue was at hand. The former, he supposed, was the only real prospect; only the foolhardy would advocate initiating a search in such conditions.

Sandy Hoynes, still trying to recover himself, reached into the bib of his dungarees and fished out his pipe and tobacco. Soon the wheelhouse was clouded by pungent smoke as he puffed away.

He was just beginning to feel at peace when a flash of something to port was caught in the light of the sea lantern.

# 21

Kinloch's town hall was thronged with people. Provost McMurdo stood on the dais, held out his hands and called to quieten the loud chatter. Gradually, the din diminished to a low murmur. He looked around the townsfolk who had gathered at this early hour to work out just what was to be done to find the *Girl Maggie*. Many of them had been listening to the wireless appeals, and they were now anxious for news.

'Ladies and gentlemen,' began McMurdo, 'I know how worried you are about our missing friends. But rest assured that all that is humanly possible is being done to locate them.'

'The lifeboat's still at the new quay. They'll no' find them there,' scoffed Peeny, a look of disgust on his face.

'In all conscience – and after discussion with the crew and the Coastguard – I cannot ask the lifeboat to take to sea in these conditions.'

'But you didna bother aboot sending the fleet oot in it yesterday,' an elderly woman shouted from the back of the hall. She was wrapped in an ancient greatcoat, brandishing a cigarette like a rapier in front of her as she spoke.

'We had no idea how long this would last. The forecast was for the snow to clear. But as you can all see, it hasn't.' McMurdo nodded across to the arched windows through which the snow could be viewed still falling heavily under the pale glow of the street lamps.

'Huh!' replied the woman with disgust. 'It's easy seen you're a man. If I was tae hang oot my washing every time the weather forecast tells me things are improving, there'd no' be a stitch o' dry clothes in the hoose!' This garnered general agreement.

An old man in a wheelchair raised a withered, bony finger and directed it towards McMurdo. 'You've sent fine men tae their maker. The blame is yours and nobody else's. It's a fact for which there is no excuse.'

'Aye, the blood's soaked right intae your simmet,' said McKirdy with a shake of the head. 'There's no' a mair respected man than Sandy Hoynes.'

At this a hush descended on the hall.

'Well, I widna quite say that,' said Jim McCahill. 'He sails right close tae the wind at the best o' times.'

'Aye, but we've a' cut corners here and there,' said McKirdy.

'He sold me a set o' nets that weren't fit for burning,' piped up a young man in a sou'wester.

'And they say he filled a box of fish wae sand to up the weight,' shouted another. 'Right doon the gobs o' the poor creatures, tae. It's a sin tae treat a fish like that – deid, or no'.'

'He telt me he'd seen a mermaid sunning herself on the barrel rocks,' shouted a cross-eyed man. 'Even telt me she had blue hair and a fine bust – if yous don't mind me bringing up such a thing.'

'You canna blame a man for taking the rise oot o' you, Peter,' said Peeny. 'Who on earth would believe that?'

'Me!' replied Peter indignantly.

'I heard he's got a woman on board!' shouted a man in a thick blue sweater.

'Aye, I heard that,' said McKirdy.

'Likely he's floatin' aboot wae a harem. I mean, that would explain why Hamish has no lassie in tow. All sorts could be going on when he goes tae sea that we've no notion of.'

McMurdo held out his hands again like a minister about to lead his congregation in prayer. 'Come, ladies and gentlemen, let's not turn this into a forum for idle gossip. The lives of men are at stake here.'

'Aye, and a woman by the sound o' it,' said McKirdy.

'To the matter in hand.' McMurdo decided it was time to bring the meeting to order. 'It will be light in a couple of hours. Our friends in the Coastguard and the Royal Navy will guide us as to when it's best to begin a proper search. In the meantime, we should all think of those aboard the *Girl Maggie* and pray to God that Sandy Hoynes knows his stuff.'

Everyone nodded, and the hall fell silent.

❄

For a few moments, time seemed to stop in the wheelhouse of the *Girl Maggie*. Hoynes was holding the pipe in one hand, his mouth agape. He could see more of the vessel now that it was athwart his port side. She was long and sleek, with a square-rigged sail. He was mesmerised, taking in the beauty of her sweeping lines through the darkness and heavy snow.

Two large sconces at either end of the craft blazed with bright flames that silhouetted those aboard. He could see that they were broad, well-built men, and counted at least twenty, peering at him as he stared at them.

Hoynes slowly emerged from the wheelhouse. For some

reason, he felt the need to raise his hands, as though in surrender. He removed the sea lantern from its hook and stared across the few feet of waves at the sleek ship shimmering in the dancing flames.

It was then that the light from his lantern caught the face of one of those on the vessel. The man was leaning on one leg, which rested on the low gunwale, a broad smile on his face. Though it was too dark to see what he was wearing, Hoynes caught the sheen of leather from his breeches and jacket, but they were of a design he had never seen.

'We are lost, you and I,' said the man casually. His voice was deep, and seemed to fluctuate in the still air. Though they were at sea, they could easily have been on a pond such was the uncanny silence.

'Aye, I'd say that few seafarers would be able to navigate through this,' Hoynes replied.

'But I think I have the advantage. Where I am from, this weather can happen in any winter.'

Hoynes was about to reply when the light from his lantern caught something else. From the curved prow of the boat, a great wooden serpent swept into the darkness. He could just about make out its pointed head, and the intricate carvings on its flanks.

'You like my boat, I can tell,' said the stranger.

'Aye. She's beautiful. Built for speed, I reckon.'

'Yes, she is fast. Her name is *Sea Storm*. She moves through the waves as no other vessel can, propelled by the greatest waves. And we sail far and wide. She is our home, our fortress – our lover. I'm sure you feel the same way about your own craft.'

Hoynes considered this. 'Aye, well, something like that, right enough.'

His opposite number spoke quickly, using words he didn't understand, and a burst of coarse laughter came from the silhouetted crew. 'I apologise. My men have an odd sense of humour.'

'The same has been said aboot mysel' right enough.' Slowly Hoynes placed his hands at his sides. He knew he should be frightened, that something here wasn't right, but he sensed no measure of threat from the men in the beautiful boat – the reverse, in fact.

'Are you willing to take advice from one man of the sea to another?'

'Aye, I am. There's an old saying where I come from: when you're lost in a storm, take any help that's forthcoming. My faither was never done saying it.'

'Then your father was a very wise man.' The man smiled and nodded, the light of Hoynes' lantern catching the gleam of his swept-back flaxen hair and the braids of his beard.

'I hope you don't mind me saying, but that's a fine set of whiskers you have, right enough. My beard's a bit on the unruly side.'

'Thank you. My wife plaits and oils it for me before each journey.'

'My wife makes me sandwiches and a flask of tea.'

The man in dark leather threw back his head and laughed heartily at this. When he recovered he stared at Hoynes, his black eyes piercing in the snow-speckled night. 'You know that it is fate that brings us together, yes?'

'I'm prepared tae believe that.'

'A great chasm of time separates us, and yet here we are. But like seeing the coast of a distant shore in the haze of a summer's day, we too can glance through time.'

'I've heard o' such a thing. There was an old fisherman I sailed with many a year ago who swore that he saw the coast o' Buenos Aires when he was on the east side o' Islay. Mind you, he took a good drink, but he was right convincing when it came tae this. Quite fractious he'd get if anyone tried tae gainsay him. Something tae dae with refraction, so they say.'

'And he was right! None of us really know what is in store. We think we are clever; we master the sea, the land – maybe even the sky one day – but to those who watch over us, we are mere playthings. It is something we should never forget. For there will come a day when man believes himself to be a god, and on that day there will be nowhere for us to go. We will cease to exit and all that will remain will be Valhalla.'

Hoynes knew he'd heard that name before. After brief consideration he reckoned it was a pub in Oban. But as he kept his visits to that place as short as he possibly could, there was no telling if his memory was playing him false. All the same, he felt it only polite to nod and smile in agreement. Though he did feel slightly disappointed that the only remnant of humanity was likely to be some run-down bar in Oban.

'I must sail on, my friend. But first I tell you this. This snow will last until the sun is high. But if you turn your vessel right round, you will be safe when it shines through the clouds. Look for a guide – a bird will point the way.'

The beautiful boat began to fade into the snowy darkness. Hoynes held the lantern higher, but it caught only ghostly shadows. 'Thank you!' he called. 'I don't even know your name.'

'My name? You know it already, I think. The part of you

that sees what can't be seen and feels what can't be felt does. Odin is with you always.' The swirling voice was distant now. 'My name is Hona, and we will meet again one day, of that you can be assured.'

Hoynes tried to speak, but no words would come.

# 22

Though dawn had broken over Kinloch it was a thin, miserable affair. The sky was still heavy with clouds, and snow fell without pause or hindrance on the town.

The Machrie miners had been back, digging deep trenches where once there had been roads and pavements. And a few hardy souls were battling through this new white-walled landscape to buy much needed groceries or just meet up for a chat in a pub or café with their fellow townsfolk. The main points of discussion were inevitably the unusual weather and the plight of the *Girl Maggie*.

The aromas of sausages cooking in Alistair the butcher's shop, hot coffee from the Italian delicatessen and warm bread being baked by Michael Kerr wafted through the passages: all overlaid, as ever, by the tang of the sea. From Kinloch's many watering holes, the mellow scent of whisky and tobacco drifted. Astute publicans, more than aware that the local police had enough to deal with, opened early, so by mid-morning the likes of the Douglas Arms and the County Hotel were thronged with customers eager for news of recent developments.

Provost McMurdo stood at his office window two floors above Main Street. To him the white pathways through the snow looked like the mazes contrived from great hedges at stately homes. He looked on as Andy Galbraith paused to remove his bunnet and scratch his head, wondering just where he was going. McMurdo had a mind to tap the window and guide him from above, but realised that, with Hoynes still missing, his standing with the local population was pretty low. There was no doubt that his idea to send the fishing fleet to Ayrshire in the midst of a blizzard was widely viewed as reckless, to say the least. The old man sensed his gaze and looked up at the office window. McMurdo could only smile politely and pretend he hadn't noticed the baleful expression on the face of Andy Galbraith.

He'd been in touch with the Royal Navy, the Coastguard and the harbour masters in both Kinloch and Girvan. The feeling was unanimous: no search could be mounted until the weather eased, and even the forecasters were unsure as to when that might be.

Miserably, he returned to his desk and took a cigar from a drawer. He knew that someone might arrive and witness his clandestine habit, but he was past caring. He was exhausted, guilt-ridden and at the end of his tether. Having been up all night, with only weak tea as a roborative, his stamina was sorely stretched.

Though he'd been brought up as a strict Presbyterian, once free from the influence of his overbearing father, in adulthood he'd let religion slide somewhat. But now, in desperation, he bowed his head and prayed that the weather would turn and Hoynes, his boat and crew would be found hale and hearty.

In the middle of his plea to the heavens, the phone on his desk burst into life. 'Hello, Provost McMurdo,' he said wearily.

'It's Donald Fletcher here. I'm the duty harbour master at Girvan.'

McMurdo sat straighter in his chair. Could this be the good news he was so desperate to hear? 'Yes, Mr Fletcher, what can I do for you? What we're looking for, I hope?'

'Well, I have to be honest, Mr McMurdo. Initially we thought it was the worst news possible.'

'Oh dear!'

'Please, stay calm while I tell you the details.'

Heart in mouth, McMurdo listened, lighting his cigar as a salve against what might come.

'About two hours ago, a gentleman reported wreckage on a beach just outside Girvan.'

McMurdo held his head in his hands.

'The timbers were definitely from a boat, but there was something unusual about their construction. They were very black. At first I thought the timbers were fire damaged, but on examination that didn't appear to be the case.'

'Well, what then?'

'We've had Mr Hart the county archaeologist take a look. He's just called me from a phone box. You'll remember we had storms a couple of weeks ago. Well, he reckons that these fragments could be hundreds of years old. The theory is they've been dislodged from the silt that preserved them by heavy seas. Had it not been for the beach being covered in snow, we may have missed them altogether. Mr Hart thinks he has part of a Viking longship – even part of the prow!'

'Well, yes, that's very exciting, but it doesn't help our missing fishing boat, does it?'

'No, I understand that. But the press have a hold of this already, and I didn't want you coming across tales of wreckage in some misleading report, if you know what I mean?'

'Ah, I see. Very considerate, thank you.'

'But there is a bit of good news, Mr McMurdo. The snow has stopped here, and the sky's clearing. We'll begin our search from this end shortly. Shouldn't be surprised if things will improve in Kintyre quite soon.'

McMurdo expressed his gratitude and ended the call. At least this was something positive. Though the story about the Viking wreckage he could have done without.

When he looked out of his office window, Kinloch's provost was sure that the falling snow looked lighter, the flakes a little smaller and less frequent. He took a deep puff on his cigar and hoped for the best.

❄

Hamish was now in the bottom bunk where not long ago Sandy Hoynes had thought himself to be a lobster. His head was aching, and he was still slightly disoriented. But Jo was clucking over him like a mother hen, supplying him with tea and even a large chunk of cheese with bread.

'You don't have tae fuss,' said Hamish. 'I've a hard heid, you know.'

'I'll be the judge of that. Now drink your tea while it's hot,' replied Jo.

'For the life of me, I canna remember how I fell. I'm usually quite sure-footed.'

As it was clear Hamish had no memory of falling due to their tussle over her bag, Jo felt it prudent not to enlighten him. 'Don't fret about it. Just rest and get yourself back together.'

'I'm fretting o'er Sandy. Are you sure he's fit to be up in the wheelhouse?'

'He's fine, quite back to normal.'

'And he doesna think he's a lobster – or any other crustacean, come to that?'

'No, he's right as rain.'

With that, Hoynes boots appeared through the hatch, shortly followed by their owner.

'Skipper! How are you faring?'

'Aye, I'm fine.'

'No notions o' shellfish at all?'

'Eh?' Hoynes looked bewildered.

'Och, never mind. It's good to see you back at the helm.' Hamish paused. 'The weather must have improved. We've got a fair shake on, by the sound o' they engines.'

'It's light, at least, but still snowing.'

'But you're ploughing on?' Hamish looked at Jo with a worried expression.

'I canna spend much time chewing the fat o'er this. But suffice it tae say I had an encounter with another mariner just before dawn. He put me right in terms of direction and the like.'

'No doubt he had radar or some such contraption?'

Hoynes inclined his head in thought. 'No, I don't think so.'

'So how did he know what directions tae gie you? Maybe news from the Coastguard on the radio?'

'Och, Hamish, man. You took a right dunt on the heid, for certain sure. He was a Viking. Men like that don't need the likes o' radio and radar. They could navigate all the way tae Greenland wae jeest a glance at the sky, and perhaps identify a bird or two on the way.' Hoynes shook his head. 'I'll need tae get back tae the wheelhouse. Just checking you were still in the land o' the living.' With that, he forced himself through the hatch and disappeared back on deck.

'Help me up!' wailed Hamish.

'You should stay where you are!' said Jo.

'The skipper's been talking tae Vikings. I'll have tae get up there and talk sense intae him!'

Jo helped Hamish to his feet and, with his arm over her shoulder, they staggered to the hatch.

'If I can get up on that chair, I'll make it.'

'Are you sure?'

'It's that or a watery grave. Which dae you fancy?'

Jo rushed to get the chair.

# 23

With Jo's help, Hamish managed to manoeuvre himself through the hatch and onto the deck. The snow was deeper than ever, reaching almost halfway up his wellington boots, but he reckoned that even though the visibility was still awful, at least the flakes had reduced in size. For Hamish, this was a sure sign that the general situation was improving. Though he was dismayed to note that the *Girl Maggie* was hammering on at not far off her top speed. A great plume of black smoke belching from the thin funnel attached to the side of the wheelhouse bore testament to this.

Hoynes was at the wheel, pipe gripped between his teeth, staring grimly into the white wall of falling snow.

Though his head was thumping, Hamish realised that it was prudent to take a circuitous route in terms of expressing any concerns about their present rate of travel. Hoynes, at the best of times, was a man over-proud of his skills as a mariner. But Hamish wasn't convinced that the advice of a passing Viking should be followed under these circumstances – or any circumstances, come to that.

'You've got a fair head o' steam on, skipper. Man, we must be hitting near ten knots.'

'Aye, despite the snow, the boat's sailing like a dream. A wee bit low in the water, mind you, but that's tae be expected, what wae a' this weight we're carrying. Heavier than a hold filled tae the brim wae fish, Hamish.'

Hamish swallowed hard before making a suggestion. 'Sandy, dae you no' think we should haul her back a fraction? It's hellish hard tae see anything. Visibility must be only a few yards, and that's no' telling you o'er much.'

Hoynes removed the pipe from between his teeth and addressed his first mate in a restrained, but determined manner. 'I've been set a course by a man who knew fine what he was at. I've nae reason at all tae doubt the information. My, if you'd seen him yourself, you'd be fair ploughing on like I am.'

Hamish cleared his throat. 'Sandy, you've no' been yourself in the last wee while.'

'No' myself? What on earth are you blethering aboot?'

'It kind o' began when you saw fit tae chase thon giant lobster aboot the deck wae a boat hook. Something wisnae jeest quite right, you understand.'

'And what did I do then? Maybe a pirouette roon the stern?'

'No, no' quite, Sandy. In fact, you ended up thinking you were a lobster yourself. Fair snapping your fingers together like claws, you were. I managed tae get a few words from you aboot it all, but maybe we should consign that to the past.'

Hoynes looked at Hamish in disbelief. 'I can see a lump the size o' a duck egg emerging through what's left o' your hair. You need to get yourself back doon intae the warmth o' that bunk.'

'There's no need tae be so personal,' said Hamish, who was most self-conscious that his hair wasn't as lustrous as it once had been.

'I've been on the water since I was a babe in arms. When the old king was no more than a midshipman. Aye, and I've sailed

132

under some o' the best skippers there's ever been. Not tae mention my own late lamented faither. He could navigate his way tae Mars if the equipment was available tae perform such a journey.'

They were both startled by the sound of a massive gull squawking loudly as it swept over the vessel.

'That must be the biggest seagull I've yet tae set eyes on,' said Hamish. 'A junior albatross, I shouldna be surprised.'

'No such thing. An albatross has an altogether different cant tae its wings, and an entirely different beak. Man, Hamish, your ornithological observation leaves a lot tae be desired, and you a man o' the sea. I'll tell you what it is.'

'What?'

'It's a sign. My Viking friend telt me that it would arrive in good time.'

The gull was now flying a few feet above and to the front of the *Girl Maggie*. It wheeled in the air and Sandy Hoynes spun the wheel to follow its course.

'There we are. Good as gold. Och, we'll be in Girvan before you can say, "Old McKirdy's a right miserable bugger."'

'Sandy, as first mate of this vessel, I must register my opposition to your present course o' action!'

Hoynes pursed his lips and glared at Hamish. 'You try any o' that Fletcher Christian stuff and I'll gie you another dunt on the heid wae this boat hook. I'm the captain o' this vessel. No jeest that, I'm its owner intae the bargain. One day you'll have your own boat to command. In the meantime, pipe doon and away and get me a hot mug o' tea. Fair parched, I am.'

Hamish shrugged and made his way back through the hatch and into the cabin.

'Any luck?' said Jo.

'Are you a religious person at all?' asked Hamish.

'No, not particularly. Why?'

'Well, if I was you, I'd try to find some o' it as quick as you can muster. For not only are we following the nautical suggestions o' a Viking, we're now taking the navigational advice o' a gull.'

'That's not good, is it?'

'Aye, you could put it in those terms. Then again, you could be much mair strident.'

'So what do we do?'

'We get some life jackets on, go up on deck, brace ourselves and hope for the best.'

❄

First of all, the skies over Kinloch brightened slightly, although the snow still fell. But soon it began to slow, and before long only the odd small flake added to the great mounds of white that covered the place.

In his office, McMurdo looked to the sky, relief spread across his face. He knew that they were a long way from finding the *Girl Maggie* and her crew, but at least this was a start. Soon, perhaps, they could launch a search in earnest.

He was about to call the harbour master when a tiny square of blue sky appeared through the snow clouds. It sent a shaft of light onto the street below that would have looked heavenly had it not been for the fact that it landed on the town clerk as he made his way back from Michael Kerr's with some bacon rolls.

Within the space of a quarter of an hour, phone calls were made, and McMurdo sat back at his desk with a strong cup of tea, savouring the taste and smell of crispy bacon. Lifeboats from Kinloch and Girvan had been launched, and a Royal Navy destroyer was steaming down the Clyde to assist with the search.

Kinloch's provost closed his eyes in a silent prayer. Hoynes was a rather prickly man to deal with, and a highly vocal member of the community who often disagreed with the decisions of the town council, but at this very moment there was no other face he'd rather see.

# 24

Hamish and Jo were now huddled on deck in stout yellow lifejackets. Hoynes stared at them from the wheelhouse with barely disguised contempt. 'For the life o' me, I canna understand why two almost sensible folk would choose tae shiver on deck when there's a nice warm cabin below.'

'Because we want tae be ready tae dive intae the sea if you hit they rocks,' said Hamish, quite mutinous now. He was, though, slightly taken aback by the big gull. It had held its position above the bow and was flapping as determinedly as ever, with what seemed to Hamish like clear intent. But such was the mood of the *Girl Maggie*'s first mate at this time of great anxiety that he saw the intent as malign, perhaps even murderous in nature.

Jo, who'd been watching him stare at the bird, cocked her head. 'They say that animals and birds have a sixth sense that we don't have.'

'Fish don't. They're right stupid creatures,' Hamish replied.

'But that's not a flying fish, it's a gull. Looks to me as though it knows what it's about.'

Hamish looked taken aback. 'I'm no' quite sure jeest what has got into you and the skipper. But whatever it is, I wish it would desist.'

'No, honestly, you read about these things all the time. In fact we covered a story in the paper last year. A man out swimming somewhere off Mull got out of his depth. He was tiring, trying to make for the shore with the tide against him. Out of nowhere this pod of dolphins surrounded him and pushed him to the shore. You know, like a strong wind.'

'Sounds mair to me like strong drink was involved, if you don't mind me saying. I read the other day that they'd have men walking on the moon before the decade is oot. Sheer nonsense! Look at the state *we're* in, and that's on account of a bit of snow between Kinloch and Girvan. Imagine the horrors they'd encounter on the way tae the moon.'

'They'll make it, don't you worry.'

'Aye, they'll make it up, likely. Some clever studio in Hollywood will pitch in and make gullible folk believe anything. It's all jeest one-upmanship wae they Russians.'

Jo grabbed Hamish's arm. 'Look!' she said, pointing upwards.

Sure enough, a small patch of blue had appeared amongst the snow clouds. It was tiny, but seemed to be growing. The snow, too, was turning into nothing more than a flurry.

'Sandy!' shouted Hamish. 'The weather's clearing.'

Hoynes stuck his head from the wheelhouse and stared at the patch of blue. 'Aye, and you wae no faith in Vikings – or gulls, come tae that.'

With that, the gull soared away and was soon lost in what was left of the cloud.

'Bugger,' said Hoynes under his breath.

'Land ahoy!' shouted Hamish. He was sharper-eyed than Hoynes, for soon a great white loom that definitely wasn't sea or sky began to appear through the tiny specks of snow.

'Ach,' said Hoynes, 'there we are. That's the hill that overlooks Girvan harbour, if I'm no' much mistaken.'

A shaft of bright sunlight suddenly broke through the clouds, illuminating the ghostly land like some huge spotlight.

'Never mind the hill at Girvan, Sandy. We're at the mouth o' the loch.'

'Which loch?' Hoynes looked on with a puzzled expression.

'Our ain – Kinloch – can you no' see it, man?'

As Hoynes stared, his eyes widened. Sure enough, the island at the head of the loch was to his left, the red and green buoys marking the channel into the their home port.

'Wow!' said Jo.

'It's a miracle,' Hamish remarked.

'It's no surprise tae me at all,' said Hoynes. He slowed the *Girl Maggie* and made his way confidently between the buoys, taking time to tamp some tobacco into his pipe and puff it into life with two flaring matches.

'What dae you mean, "no surprise"? You thought we were just about tae make port at Girvan!' said Hamish.

'I was just having you on. Man, you're a serious cove, right enough. It would be madness to have stayed on course for Girvan. Jeest ask Hona.'

'Who?'

'Hona the Viking. I'm sure I told you all about it.'

As the crew of the *Girl Maggie* argued back and forth, Jo disappeared. A few minutes later, she popped back up through the hatch, this time with her camera. It looked huge in her small hands as she framed shots and snapped away. 'What a story this is going to make!' she exclaimed, as Kinloch came into view at the end of the bay.

'Aye, but me and you will have tae have a word aboot that,' said Hoynes.

✻

McMurdo's phone rang. He picked it up quickly, anxious for news. Kinloch was now bathed in bright winter sunshine, making the snow that had fallen on the town sparkle like a glittering Christmas card.

'They're sailing into the loch,' said Mitchell, the harbour master.

'Who, Hoynes?' McMurdo could hardly believe his ears.

'Aye, plain as day. The lifeboat must have passed them in the snow. For they've not seen head nor tail of them since they ventured out earlier. I'm away to bring them back in.'

'Excellent! Thank you, Mr Mitchell.' Before he heard a reply, McMurdo slammed the phone back into its cradle and pulled on his overcoat. Soon he was making his way towards the quay, and although he slipped and fell a couple of times, the ache in his knee and loss of pride barely registered, as the vista opened out by the head of the loch.

Sure enough, only a hundred or so yards from the harbour mouth the *Girl Maggie* could be seen, black smoke issuing from her funnel.

McMurdo came to a halt beside Peeny and McKirdy.

'I knew fine he would make it,' said Peeny. 'The man's a genius wae navigation and the like.'

'Aye, through one o' the worst snow storms in history tae,' said McKirdy. He looked at Kinloch's provost, who was now wearing a broad smile under his trilby. 'You'll be mighty relieved, I'm thinking, eh?'

'Of course,' said McMurdo.

'Aye, they'd likely have burned you at the stake if she'd been lost at sea.'

'A tragic thought, but thankfully avoided. Don't you think you're being a touch melodramatic, McKirdy?'

'This is Kinloch. You should know that by now.' At his side, Peeny nodded his head.

On the pier, a huge cheer broke out from those who had been keeping up a silent vigil for the return of Hoynes and his vessel.

❈

On board the *Girl Maggie*, Jo had been ordered below, much against her will, it had to be said. Hoynes was more than aware that the presence of a woman on his boat would be seen as the tempting of fate that precipitated near calamity.

He stood in the wheelhouse, ready to bask in the best wishes of his townsfolk. 'Get down below and make sure young Jo knows what she's aboot, Hamish,' said Hoynes.

'Tell me again, skipper.'

'We'll tie up at the pier. While they're securing the ropes, I'll engage everyone with tales of our deliverance fae certain disaster.'

'You're no' going tae mention the Viking, are you – nor the gull?' Hamish blinked at his skipper.

For some reason, as the sky had cleared, so had the fog that clouded Hoynes' mind. He remembered being utterly convinced that he'd seen and spoken to the Viking. But now it was like a dream. 'I think we'll no' say much aboot that at the moment. Maybe jeest touch on my skills at navigation. As for the gull, well, there's nothing wrong wae that. He jeest happened to be heading in the same direction as ourselves. The creature likely recognised my determination, hence he took oor lead towards home.'

'Aye, but he was taking the lead, Sandy.'

'But I saw him looking back oot the corner o' his eye tae see where I was at. Clever creatures, they gulls. If I'd steered a degree away, that bird would have altered his course.'

'If you'd steered away, we'd have been on the rocks at the island, Sandy.'

'Well, I didna. Now, make sure your wee friend gets kitted oot in a bunnet and dungarees that'll make her look sufficiently like a cabin boy. When I alight on the pier, I'll lead everyone up tae the County. No doubt there will be the usual questions and wonder at oor skill in making port in such conditions. When the coast is clear, you and Jo can make a break for it. She's crafty enough, o' that there's no' much doubt.'

'And if she's no' of a mind tae align wae your thinking, Sandy?'

'That's what first mates are for, Hamish. I've every faith you'll use your charm to persuade her that this is the only sensible course o' action. After all, she'll have surely taken a fancy to such a well set-up chap like yourself. Fair heroic you are now, intae the bargain.'

As Hoynes watched Hamish head back to the cabin below, he was sure he'd flattered his first mate sufficiently to ensure he'd get the job done.

Expertly he slowed the *Girl Maggie* to a stop by the pier, and the fleet-footed harbour master jumped aboard with a rope to secure her to the quayside.

High above them in the clear blue sky, a gull circled, one eye cocked with interest on the events unfolding in the harbour below.

# 25

Hoynes was amidst a gaggle of folk, all interested to hear about his deliverance from the blizzard that should have made navigation – especially without the aid of radio and radar – impossible.

Hoynes stood, his boots planted firmly in the snow, smoke from his pipe billowing over the crowd. 'Well, you see, after a number of years on the great ocean, a mariner gets a notion – an instinct, if you fancy – aboot jeest where he is in the world. For myself, I think it's a skill bred intae us seamen, the same as it is wae salmon, pigeons and the like.'

'A lot o' pish,' said McKirdy under his breath.

'Moreover, when danger beckons, the sea looks after those who looked after it. Mother Nature's no' wanting the likes o' radar and such contraptions upsetting the balance o' things. It's all mair a cock o' the heid here and a sniff o' the wind there. I'm sure you all know what I mean.'

'I'm sniffing plenty wind right at the moment,' whispered Peeny.

'So, Mr Hoynes, would you say you were guided by the spirits of the sea?' This from McMahon, the young reporter from the *Kinloch Herald* whose prominent front teeth always made him look inquisitive.

'You could say that. Alternatively, you could say that a higher hand guided me through the perils o' the last few hours o' great darkness and despair.'

At this point, raised voices could be heard from the *Girl Maggie*. As Hoynes extolled the virtue of good seamanship in tandem with heavenly intervention, they became more pronounced.

'Is there a problem on the boat?' asked McMurdo.

'Och no, it's jeest Hamish letting off steam. You know the perilous state o' young folk these days. All kinds o' nonsense spinning aboot their heids.'

'I can hear two voices,' said McKirdy, a knowing look on his face.

'Me tae,' agreed Peeny.

'He does that sometimes,' said Hoynes. 'A hell of a man for the impersonations. He does a great Harold McMillan, though his Andy Stewart could do wae a bit o' work, right enough.'

As the voices on Hoynes' vessel became louder, everyone's attention was now diverted.

'Let's leave Hamish tae his nonsense and head up for a cosy dram and a chat in the County. I'm fair gasping for a glass o' whisky after all these trials and tribulations, no doubt about it.'

At that, a figure emerged through the hatch of the *Girl Maggie*. At first, with a greasy bunnet pulled down over the face, it looked for all the world like a small boy. But as a hand appeared and grabbed at the boy's ankle the bunnet was dislodged, revealing a young woman with a fashionably bobbed haircut.

'Just let me go, Hamish!' shouted Jo, as a collective gasp issued from those on the pier.

'Aye,' said McKirdy. 'I knew it fine. A woman, plain as day. No wonder you were lost at sea, Sandy Hoynes!'

'Och, I can explain,' said Hoynes, as Hamish emerged looking fretful.

'I'll explain, if someone will help me off this bloody tub!' Jo exclaimed.

Willing hands breached the space between the vessel and the pier, gently hauling the young woman in the ill-fitting dungarees up from the *Girl Maggie*, as Hoynes looked on, a resigned look on his face.

'I'm a reporter from the *Glasgow Times*,' said Jo. 'Mr Hoynes entered into a bona fide contract with the paper, so that we might cover his mercy mission to feed the stranded community here in Kinloch. But he took the money before he realised I was a woman.'

Another gasp from those gathered.

'I was fair conned intae it. Aye, and Hamish here is by no means without blame,' Hoynes remonstrated.

'Hold on, skipper,' said Hamish. 'You jeest misunderstood what was happening.'

A woman's voice piped up, this time from the back of the assembly. 'You telt me this lassie had a broken leg, Sandy Hoynes!'

'Mother!' Hamish wailed. 'What are you doing here?'

'What kind o' a mother would I be if I didna come to greet my own son, saved from a watery grave? But you'll wish you were in one if I hear there's been any shenanigans aboard that vessel.'

'Shenanigans!' said Hoynes. 'I'll have you know that no such things took place on the *Girl Maggie*.'

'Too right,' said Jo. 'Hamish is a nice enough man, but he's not my type.'

'I telt you he'd missed the boat as far as a wife was concerned,' said McKirdy.

Hoynes called for order. 'I'll admit I was mistaken in taking the young lassie aboard. But, as I say, I was misled.'

'Tell them how I saved your precious boat,' said Jo.

'You jeest get back to your work. You'll have plenty tae type up, and no mistake,' said Hoynes, in an effort to silence the reporter.

'I'll not be hushed up like some child. The truth is that both Mr Hoynes and Hamish were indisposed. It was up to me in the middle of the night to save the vessel.'

'Huh! As we thought, the pair of them fair steaming, thinking they had nothing to lose. Shame on you, Sandy Hoynes,' said Peeny.

'I'll have you know I was not drunk. I was rendered insensible by a hallucinogenic!'

This statement silenced everyone present.

'He thought he was a lobster,' said Hamish from the deck of the *Girl Maggie*.

'I think we've heard enough,' said McMurdo. 'I'm sure the harbour master will enquire further as to what happened aboard your vessel, Mr Hoynes. It all sounds most irregular to me. I'm quite sure a number of breaches of maritime law have been committed.'

'Off his heid on the drugs! Aye, the whole town will be a laughing stock when this emerges,' said McKirdy.

'Let me explain!' Hoynes shouted, but to no avail.

In dribs and drabs, the impromptu welcoming committee made their way back to the snowy town, many shaking their heads at the shame of it all.

'Well, thank you very much,' said Hoynes to Jo.

'Stop your grumbling. We'd be at the bottom of the sea – and you know it – had I not tied that wheel to make the boat turn in circles.'

'And whose fault was that?'

'You put the sugar lump in your own tea,' said Jo. 'Anyway, don't worry about that. I'll say in my report that you ate some dodgy shellfish.'

'No' lobster, mind,' said Hamish.

Shaking his head, Hoynes turned on his heel and marched up the pier, only to slip outside the weigh house and collide with a bollard. Despite this setback, he picked himself up, dusted himself down, and was soon lost in the snow-packed trenches that were the streets of Kinloch.

# Epilogue

In the days that followed, outrage subsided when Jo Baird's article appeared in the *Glasgow Times*. The people of Kinloch read it a day late, the papers and vital supplies having to be brought aboard a MacBrayne's ferry.

Though Peeny and McKirdy swore that Hoynes was a martyr to narcotics, most settled for Jo's explanation that he'd been poisoned by shellfish. She was unrepentant as to the role she'd played in saving the vessel, and soon the general feeling was that it was high time the ridiculous superstition that women had no place on boats be crushed once and for all.

After many trials, Hamish succeeded in convincing his mother that nothing untoward had passed between him and the pretty young reporter. Soon, the events of the blizzard melted away with the snow that had isolated the town.

❋

Sandy Hoynes, though, was still troubled. The nagging memory of the Viking who had been their salvation lingered on his mind. But he managed to persuade himself that it had merely been his subconscious dealing with matters in hand while still under the influence.

When Christmas and New Year were past, and strong gales were battering Kinloch, looking for a diversion before the County Hotel opened, Hoynes made his way to the local library.

'I'm wondering,' he enquired of Mrs Duncan the librarian. 'Have you anything on Vikings – particularly any known to have frequented our own coastline?'

'I can find you some good books on the subject, Mr Hoynes. But, as it happens, I have always had an interest in the Northmen myself. In fact, we had our very own Viking lord. He died at the Battle of Largs, but by all accounts – and one has to take them with a pinch of salt, of course – he was a bit of a character. Had land up near Firdale. Hona was his name, though his nickname was The Serpent. Apparently the prow of his boat was carved into a likeness of the creature. Lovely story, but likely just myth.' She smiled. 'In fact, if you give me a moment, I have a wee pamphlet I wrote on the subject. The engraving on the cover was taken from a woodcut found at Edail Abbey. But, like the story, possibly a construction of many years later.'

Hoynes stared at the book, wide-eyed. Though crudely drawn, there was the man who'd pointed his way to salvation in the snow. The sleeked-back flaxen hair, the clothes – everything was as Hoynes remembered. 'In my opinion, Mrs Duncan, no myth.' He turned round slowly and walked away. 'I'll come back for the books tomorrow.'

Hoynes paused outside the library and stared across the loch, the wind tugging at his pea jacket. 'More things in heaven and earth, right enough,' he muttered to himself before shuffling away, quite bemused.

❄

High above the town, where the ramparts of the old hill fort had once stood, sat the gull, the soul of Kinloch. Head to one side, he watched the distant figure of Hoynes as he made his way along the esplanade.

With a loud squawk, he spread his great wings and soon was soaring on the strong wind above the old town, over which he'd watched for so long.